# CHA SPIRITS

GW01048663

# GLYNN
# JAMES

*[signature]* Jan 2011

ISBN-13: 978-1463552572
ISBN-10: 1463552572

For Erin

# 1

I was born four seconds before the strike of midnight, on the 31st December 1900. As far as I know that makes me the last person to be born in that century. My mother, god bless her soul, she may well have been the first person to die in the century that followed, because no sooner had I taken my first breath than she took her last.

My name is Reginald Joseph Weldon or Reg if you want. That's what most folks call me. I've lived through and fought in two world wars, and I've loved just one woman in my life, just one.

I met her the night before my eighth birthday, and that brief meeting was only one of the events that set my life hurtling on a course that I'd never expected, though it was certainly the only good one, but I will get to all of that soon enough. There are too many other things I need to say.

It's 2002 now, so they tell me, 2002. It's hard to believe, isn't it? A whole new century came and went, without as much as a wave. If we're counting, then that makes me a hundred and one years old, and well, there doesn't seem to be much else to do at my age but count the days.

It seems strange to me that it has taken over a hundred years to arrive at a place in my life where I find it necessary that someone else knows about some of the things that I've come to know.

As I lie in my bed at night, in this hospital, I wonder how many days, or even hours I have left to tell my tales to whoever may one day hear them. It doesn't really matter though, just so long as I get to say everything I need to say.

Get it all out.

I couldn't write any of it down, not now. My hands just don't do what they are told to do these days. It's arthritis, apparently. That's what the doctors say. It must have crept in over the years without me noticing it.

I did try writing, even bought a brand new pen and a journal and all that, but my hands hurt a lot, especially when it's cold. You know, I still remember a time when the cold didn't mean anything to me.

So I bought this new Dictaphone tape thing. It cost a small fortune. One of the nurses, Emma I think her name is, was kind enough to pick it up for me, said she was going to the electronics store anyway. I'm not sure if she was. I think that maybe she was just being nice.

They call it Angel Ward, and do you know, I couldn't think of a more apt name than that. On this ward, all they really do is spend their time easing the way out for those of us who won't be leaving here alive.

Angels, every one of them.

Why did I wait so long to say anything? What possessed me to hide everything away without speaking a word, right up until death was taking its first glances at me? I don't know really, but I do know that my time is nearing an end. I can feel it approaching as the days pass, a light caress as I lay sleeping, a sharp nudge as I'm sitting up trying to eat, and a lingering glance as I struggle on my way to the lounge for my afternoon read. It's always there, waiting, just waiting, always ready to remind me that it won't be long now.

Not long at all.

I don't think we ever really expect our time here to end, I know that I never have. Maybe that's it. Until a few weeks ago when they told me what was happening to me, that things were going to go bad, and pretty fast as well, I had never even considered that one day it would all be over. I always believed I would get my chance again, and that I wouldn't miss it this time.

I would be ready next time.

I remember a lot of things about my life, and most of those memories are vivid, like they happened only a few days ago. I think that must be my gift. We all have a gift don't we? Something we excel at, though I think not everybody discovers what that gift may be.

There is one anomaly in my memories though, one area of my life that I don't recall so well, and that is my first few years. I remember where I was born, but I don't remember much about the place.

The village was called Temperance, and it was a tiny place, just a few miles off what is now the M1 motorway, in Northamptonshire, tucked away in that ambling countryside, that for most folks just drifts past you through a car window.

Don't ask me to tell you about how that place was back then, I spent a grand total of twelve months there, oblivious to the world as all newly born are, before my aunt took me all the way to London to live with her new husband, and that city is where I spent most of my childhood, most of my life, really. The town I was born in, and how it was before the war, is a very vague memory, and it would be so many long years before I went back there once more.

I do remember that my father didn't stay around for very long after I was born. I like to think he loved my mother too much to be able to cope with facing me once she was gone, but honestly, from the small amount I've been able to gleam about him, from odd tales that I've discovered in passing conversation with people who once knew him, I think that he just up and went, and was glad to see the back of the both of us.

Before my aunt died, when I was five years old, she told me that my mother was probably the nicest, happiest person that ever graced god's earth, and that I was an almost identical image of her. I never knew her, and I don't even remember her face, hell, I only shared this planet with my mother for barely a few seconds, but I do know I never heard of anyone that people liked more.

I do have a picture of her, a very old one that has become worn and faded over the years, but the face looking back at me doesn't trigger any memories.

During my early years I was a trouble maker of the worst kind. I had an attitude, to say the least. Where that came from I don't know. Maybe one of those psychiatrist types would have an idea, but all I know is I was an angry child, always on the look-out for trouble. And I can tell you this, that when you go around looking for it, as I did for most of my early life, you certainly find it.

I spent most of my younger years, the ones that followed the death of my aunt, hopping from one home to another, obliviously moving from one family to the next, and leaving a trail of destruction behind me. I didn't pick up many friends along the way, only a big, long line of folks who were probably glad to see me gone, and not just a few that might have liked to have seen something bad happen to me. It wasn't until the safety of a home and a family was taken away that my ways changed.

# 2

One afternoon, not many days before my eighth birthday, in December of 1908, my life changed. It happened so fast that it took me a few days just for my head to catch up. One moment I had been happily sitting there, thinking the random thoughts of a child, and the next, a world far darker had descended upon me. It was the first time I had ever had to run for my life. It certainly wouldn't be the last, but at barely eight years old you are neither expecting such a thing, nor are you prepared for it.

It was a year of bad weather where I lived at the time, just south of London in a town called Hilmoor. I remember the snow blizzards as clearly as if it had happened just yesterday, they seemed like they were ten feet tall, though I doubt that was the reality.

I was living with a family who were related to me in some way, I think they were distant cousins, though I couldn't be sure of that. I was never told.

For the first time I seemed to have settled in quite nicely. I got on well with their two sons - both of them were a few years older than me, but I tagged along and joined in with whatever games they decided we were going to play each day, and they didn't seem to mind a little kid following them around.

The game they liked to play the most was called

"who did it", a tricky game for a child of my age, I thought, and don't know which of the boys invented it, or if they had learned it from someone else, but I had never played it before.

It involved everyone sitting on the ground, facing each other with a bunch of objects placed in the middle, just within reach. It didn't matter what they were so long as they were small enough to fit in your hand. Rocks, pencils, apples, twigs, a small toy car, anything was game.

You had to sit quite close to each other so that everybody could touch the knees of those around them, and on a count of three everybody had to close their eyes.

Next came the part I couldn't get, at least not at the start. You see the whole point of the game was to take stuff, and to take it without anybody noticing you had taken it. If you noticed someone taking something, you called out their name and said "put that back!" and everyone would open their eyes, and you put back whatever you had in your hand. When everything was gone from the middle, you counted up what you had taken, and the person with the most won.

I took me a long time to figure out that both the other boys didn't close their eyes all the way, they were just squinting. Every time I took something I got called out and every time they took something I never noticed. I didn't suspect at all that they might be cheating, but then I hadn't figured out that the whole point of the game was to fool the others. It was all about deception.

We played that game most days, for hours sometimes, and somewhere along the way I started to notice things. When one of the brothers would move to take something there was a rustle of clothes, or I'd feel the air move. I started to call them out. The more I played the game, the better I got at taking stuff. But I learned to fool them in a different way. When I took something I took more than one thing, and when I got called out I put one thing back and dropped another thing neatly in the pile behind me.

Deception has many forms.

Soon I began to win every game, and the brothers started to get irritated by that. I loved that game so much, I found myself cheating so that I would lose and let them win.

I think I learned some of my most valuable lessons sitting on the ground out in the back yard with the brothers, playing that game. How the mind could be tricked so easily if you just thought a little out of the box, how you could make someone notice something with the slightest of gestures.

The week before my ordeal it had snowed so hard that we couldn't find a patch of ground dry enough and we had to find something else to do. So we made an igloo. Well, at least they called it an igloo. In truth it was really just a hole in the snow, with the sides made hard by patting them down with our gloves. We had borrowed a few pairs of their father's work gloves for the job, though I'm not sure he knew about that. Anyway, we dug into the snow about five feet, and made ourselves a little snug den in there. We tried putting a roof of snow on it but it kept on collapsing in on us.

You know that just a few months ago I watched a television programme about Eskimos, and how they make their homes, those real igloos. Well, I laughed until I cried as it reminded me of the igloo we made, and I wondered if the Eskimos really lived in those igloos, or if it was just something traditional that had turned into an art form. Wish I'd known about making snow bricks way back in 1908.

Alexander, who was the older of the two brothers, found a piece of wood to lay on the floor, and some sack cloth from their father's workshop, and we laid out the place like a little house, and sat playing trumps for hours on end.

The house was just on the edge of the town, which wasn't very big anyway, and the yard led to a dirt track that ran for about a quarter of a mile behind the back yards of the other houses in the same row, with tall trees and hedgerows along both sides. Our little igloo was about a hundred yards over the back fence and down that track.

I didn't learn what it was that their father did for a living until the day after we made that igloo. He seemed to meet a lot of people in his workshop, which was a brick-built affair, right at the bottom of their yard, with a sheet-metal roof that was rusted and near to collapsing in. We were never allowed in that workshop, though the folks he dealt with often arrived in a wagon, or on foot, to meet him at the back gate and head into the workshop to discuss whatever it was they talked about.

Most of the time they left carrying some case or sack, and looking quite happy with themselves. But on rare occasions, if you hung around outside the yards, in the alleyway you could hear them haggling over money, or arguing about something.

The boys' father, who I was told I had to call Mr Holcroft, was a harsh man with a taste for whiskey, and you could smell it on his breath pretty much all of the time. I don't think he liked me very much. He always complained about having another kid to feed, and how they barely had the money to pay for their own kids. I heard him and his wife arguing occasionally about it. He was usually complaining, and she was telling him that it wouldn't be for long, she was just helping out her friend in the city for a while.

Truth was, over the months I was there, the conversations that I heard changed somewhat. She started off on the defence, but eventually she began agreeing with him, and then the conversations stopped entirely. Though I felt as settled as I had ever been, I was aware that my stay there would not be a long one.

Over the week before, there was a lot of business being done out of that back yard. I think that Mr Holcroft had chosen the wrong bunch of folks to try and deal with, not that anyone he dealt with was the right type, because the afternoon of the day after we made the igloo, while his two sons were out with their mother, and I was the only other person around, things got a little out of hand.

I was sitting up at the top of the yard, just outside of the back door, whittling away at a piece of wood with a knife I had found in an old toolbox that summer. Some of the ground was still covered with snow, but much of it had melted over the last couple of days, and although it was cold, I still preferred to be outside than stuck in the house. I was amazed how quickly the snow had come and gone.

All over the yard was a mass of junk. There were old skeletons of machinery tools, and boxes of old metal parts of some kind. I had guessed that he liked to tinker with machinery, because he made a lot of drilling noises in that workshop. At the time I just assumed that all the stuff in the yard was just old bits that he never got round to using on his machines, or whatever he made.

Mr Holcroft didn't seem to mind us poking around in any of the stuff in the yard, so long as we never once tried to get into the workshop. One of the things I had found was my knife, stuck in the ground underneath a rusted old bucket around the back of what I think had once been a coal shed. I was surprised that neither of the other boys had found it, and kept it to myself, hidden in my boot, or at the bottom of the dresser next to my bed.

That knife had a wicked-looking blade with a bone handle. At least I think it was bone. It certainly looked it. The blade was curved in a way that I had not seen before, almost like it was made the wrong way round. It had a thick, cracked leather holder that even had a hook to attach onto a belt, if you had one, and along one side of the wickedly sharp blade were small curved serrations cut out of the metal. I was as careful as anything with it, because of the way it cut through wood as though it was just a piece of fruit. I had it in my mind that it would cut through my skin just as easily.

I was trying to carve a toy knight, just like one of those medieval ones I had seen in one of Richard's comics.

Richard was the youngest son of the two, and was definitely the favourite. He was a clever kid and had taught himself to read pretty quickly, while his older brother was lazy, and could barely make out his letters. I don't think Mr or Mrs Holcroft were the slightest bit interested in the fact that I could read and write better than either of them.

Anyway, I had just finished carving what I thought looked a pretty good likeness of the helmet that the knight on the front cover of the comic wore, when the argument started down in the workshop.

Two men had arrived about an hour before, and they met Mr Holcroft at the bottom of the yard. On the way into the yard they were all smiles and handshakes, though they looked a little nervous.

One of them was a huge man with a barrel of a chest and a beard that could have been tucked into his trousers. His head was bald although I don't think he was really that old. I just remember the winter sun almost glaring off that polished head.

The other man could best be described as a weasel. He was a small, wiry man, much older I thought, and his hair was long and greasy, slicked to his skull like wet grass. His clothes were baggy, and his trousers were far too big for him, making him look almost comical when he walked.

They weren't outside for long, and although there were words spoken, from where I was sitting I couldn't hear them too well.

About an hour passed while they were in the workshop, talking. I could make out the drone of their voices, but not what they were saying. There was also that click, click of machinery noises that seemed to go with Mr Holcroft showing anybody something.

Then there was a lot of shouting. Voices started getting raised. Now I could hear the conversation quite clearly, and the two visitors weren't just arguing about the price.

"Don't you try and pull one over on me Holcroft." It was the voice of one of the visitors, though until they stepped outside I wasn't able to make out which of the pair was doing all the shouting.

"I'm not trying to, Remy, if you'd just let me explain this, then we can clear it all up."

"Clear it all up? Like the hell we can clear it all up, that's a pile of crap and broken."

"It just jammed, they do that occasionally."

"What? They do that occasionally? I haven't seen one jam before. You're pulling one on me. Look my blood is all over the place now, cut my hand on the damn thing."

"You just need to get used to them."

"Just need to get used to them? I'll show you about getting used to the damn thing."

My heart was beating at double the pace by now. There had never been trouble in Mr Holcroft's yard before, not like this. I heard a great deal of banging, and smashing of things inside the workshop, and then the doors burst open and Mr Holcroft, his clothes ripped and blood coming out of his mouth and a cut on his forehead, came running up the yard.

"Get inside boy, quickly," he shouted, to which I panicked, stuffed my knife into my boot, and then tried to scrabble into the back door, but we met in the doorway, and I was bowled over into the hallway of the house, landing flat on my back.

I turned to try and get out of his way, because it didn't seem like he cared what it was that was stopping him from escaping, only that he got away, and I was just another obstacle.

I didn't have to worry about being shoved another time, because just as he got his first foot in the door there was one almighty bang and Mr

Holcroft's face exploded all over the room. I felt a warm splattering of fresh blood, and god knows what else, speckle all over my face. It covered a lot of my clothes too. I wiped my eyes and lay there on the floor barely yards from him, watching how his body seemed to still be trying to carry on, even though his head was now almost completely blown away. It hovered there for a few seconds, his legs stumbling, and I would swear both arms reached out to break their fall when the body finally pitched forward and hit the hallway floor, sending a cloud of dust up into the air along with more of his bits, all across the wooden floor boards of the hall.

Behind him, as the dust cleared, stood the big fellow, with the first smoking gun I ever saw in my life held in his hands.

"Hey Remy. This thing works pretty good actually," he said, blowing the smoke from the two barrels and holding it up to examine it.

"Well I'll be damned. I guess Holcroft wasn't lying so much after all, too bad."

Remy, who turned out to be the gangly, little weasel fellow, peered into the hallway and grimaced at the mess that was the remains of Mr Holcroft.

"Damn, that's nasty," he said, and put his hand to his mouth, coughing.

Then he noticed me, sitting in amongst the carnage, covered in dust. I was probably looking like a frightened rabbit, but he just smiled at me, showing just two teeth on his bottom jaw and nothing else but gums.

"Are you still alive boy?" He was laughing now. "Guess you were lucky you're down there."

He was looking up at the wall behind me. I looked back, my ears still ringing, and saw that there was barely anything of the wall remaining. The shotgun blast had torn clean through the wooden panelling, even after it had gone through Mr Holcroft's head. I realised then that if I hadn't stumbled and fallen on the ground, I would have been torn apart like his head was. I would probably have been part of the mess.

"Christ Eddie, look at the damn mess you made now."

Eddie shrugged.

"What we going to do with the kid?" said the big guy. He was looking at me with his head cocked to one side.

"Go and fetch the wagon, and fast, someone might have heard."

He glared at me for a moment.

"We can't leave him here. He'll just snitch on us."

"Right, I'll be right back."

Eddie ran off down the garden in the direction of the back gate.

It didn't take them long to steal pretty much everything in Mr Holcroft's workshop, maybe ten minutes or so. Remy tied me up, just like a turkey ready for Christmas dinner, and bundled me into the back of the wagon, which Eddie had parked out in the lane, and I was soon sitting amongst piles and piles of shotguns and rifles, all taken from Mr Holcroft's workshop. I guess he did make machines after all, just not the kind that I thought he made.

It was the first time I ever remember being in a wagon, certainly in the back of one anyway. It started bumping along the dirt track, draw by two weary-looking horses that looked like they were about fit to die. I wasn't sure I liked being in a wagon very much. I could hear the two thugs in the front discussing it all. The guns weren't the only thing they were discussing.

"So what do you reckon we should do with him? The Warehouse?"

"Hmm, we could do, or we could take him down to the east side, and sell him there."

I could make out the difference in their voices easily now, and Remy didn't just look like a weasel, he sounded like I imagined a weasel would sound too.

"Serious? To the Scrubber's place maybe?"

"Why not? They're always after new kids. They pay a good price for a healthy one like that too, at least that's what I heard."

"I never liked those idiots though."

"What are you talking like that for? You just blew the brains out of a guy because one gun jammed."

"He was pulling one on us, and you know it."

"Of course he was."

"You listening in there boy?" called Remy through the grate behind the driver's seat. "You're to be cleaning chimneys in London pretty soon."

But somewhere along the way they changed their mind, and we all ended up getting out of that wagon, just around the corner from the place that they had called The Warehouse. Except it wasn't a warehouse at all, but what used to be a butchers market in London's East End. Now it had run into disrepair and been abandoned, apart from its one use, some nights of the week. On those evenings the old market was lit up again, and busy, but everyone kept it quiet and low key, because although people knew very well that it still went on behind closed doors, no one wanted anyone to know that there was a slave market right under their noses.

I was still trussed up like a prisoner, and dragged along the alleyway at the back, past the throng of street whores, homeless, and one small group of well dressed gentlemen who had no place being there at any time of the day.

Eddie had a hold of me by the back of my jacket, and his hand was a lot stronger than any resistance I might have put up. The gangly old fellow, Remy, rapped sharply on a small rickety old door that looked like it was hanging down off its hinges, and we waited for a few moments. There was a slight creak as the door opened just a few inches, and I saw a young man's face peering out from the darkness. A muffled conversation later, and then I was being dragged into the darkness of the building.

The darkness didn't last long. I think we went maybe ten yards down a corridor, past a few figures that I could barely make out, and then we emerged into what would have once been the main workhouse of the building. The dim light of the lanterns that adorned the walls of this old derelict hall were hard on my eyes.

I heard voices, many of them, and at that time I had no clue what an auction was, but later in my life I learned as much, and that's where I was barely a few hours after watching my foster father die at the brutal end of a shotgun that he had crafted with his own hands. I was at an auction that was different to most that took place in the city, this one dealt in lives, human lives, and, worst of all, it was mainly children of my age who were being sold off to the highest bidder.

As my eyes adjusted to the light I saw there were many folks standing around in that vast hall. They were all over the place, talking in quiet voices with each other between the columned eaves, or sitting on the floor swapping bank notes, or arguing.

The centre of the hall was well lit, unlike the dark corners and arches that lined the place, where folks held their secret conversations. No, instead, the middle was lit by bright lanterns, lots of them, all the better to cast a light upon the platform in the very centre, where the auctioneer stood, calling out his bids, and taking stakes from customers who preferred to sit back in the dark, unrecognised.

As I stood between my two captors, a young boy maybe a few years older than me was being held still, in the middle of the platform, by a man whose size I've rarely seen the like of since then. He was a monster of a man, and disfigured in some way that I couldn't recognise, and he didn't seem to stand right, like his bones were having trouble holding up the mass of muscle and fat that constituted his upper body.

The bids were placed, and a few minutes later the boy was taken off into the darkness, I presume to join his new master.

I thought then that my captors were pretty scary men, but they were nothing like some of the other folks that were loitering around in that place. There was one man who I am pretty sure was thinner than was possible, I could see his face and one of his arms in the lantern light, as he sat on an empty crate smoking a pipe, and watching the proceedings.

You might think it wasn't unusual for a man to be so skinny at that time, since there was a lot of poverty. But with this man it was different, his skin was paler than most, and there was a hole in the side of his cheek about the size of my fist, the skin around it dry and cracked, peeling back to reveal a grimace of teeth, and the side of his jawbone. More unsettling that that was the relative comfort he seemed to have in sitting holding his conversation with his companions, who were hidden in the darkness around him. Every time he took a puff on that pipe, smoke spewed out of the hole and drifted in a swirling column up into the darkness. To me, a hole that size in your face should have hurt, and I didn't know what was wrong with him, I didn't want to know.

We were there for maybe half an hour before I saw her for the first time, the girl who was to be my first love, my only love. I saw her for only a few minutes. They pushed her up on to the platform and she stood there with her head hung low, her arms folded tight around her middle. I could see the tears in her eyes, and sense the fear that she was so bravely fighting. For the briefest of moments she looked over at me and I didn't think I'd ever seen such a pretty face, even behind the dirt, and the tangle of her hair that hung to her waist.

The bidding was furious, with several men raising the price time after time, and others joining in, appearing from the dark corners of the hall, to join in the chaos as hands were raised faster than the auctioneer could keep track of. He was a crooked-looking man, with a balding head and lank, greasy hair. In the harsh light I could see his pale skin glistening with sweat. His eyes darted here and there as he attempted to keep track of all the bids, raising the price by what I thought were random amounts each time he pointed at another bidder, 'Gentleman' as he called them all. I remember a wave of loathing coming over me, real hatred, as I watched. There was nothing gentle about any of the men in that place.

Then it was over, almost as suddenly as it had begun. Folks stepped back into the anonymity of the shadows once more. She was taken from the platform and disappeared from my view, into the darkness. For one moment she glanced back over her shoulder, and I would swear that she looked at me once more.

Then she was gone.

It looked just like a hangman's platform to me, just like the ones I had seen in the picture books I borrowed from the brothers. I used to sit reading them on the step in the back yard. Alexander had a lot of them in a big box under his bed and he didn't mind me reading them, so long as I asked him first. I remembered the picture of a bad knight being hanged at the gallows, remembered that it chilled me to look at the picture, and I felt that same chill when I looked at the auction platform. There was even a stump of wood, near the middle, that looked like it had been cut off at about three feet. I swear that stump was the remains of the hangman's pole, or whatever it was called. I also believe, even now, that the dark stains on the wooden boards were blood, or something else left behind when someone was hanged.

I had seen at least six or seven children, mostly older than me, step up, or be pushed up, onto that platform, before she had been taken up there. She vanished into the shadows, pulled along by the man who had bought her, a tall, thin gaunt man who I thought looked like the wind could snap him in two, like he was ill with some wasting disease.

I decided that this was not a place I liked, or a life that I wanted. I was only very young, but after moving from house to house and family to family and seeing all manner of folks, and their different, quirky ways, I was worldly enough to realise that what was happening to me was not a good thing. I had to leave very quickly, right now, if I could. There was no way I wanted to find out where I was to be dragged off to next.

Eddie still had a hold of me very tight, his grasp like an iron weight on my shoulder, fingers digging into the soft bit of flesh underneath my collar, but the ropes they had secured me with had been left to loosen during the journey, and with a little shuffling I managed to let them drop at my feet. They hadn't tied them very well. I guess they didn't expect me to struggle. In a few minutes I was able to step over the rope and free myself without them noticing. I gave the rope a little flick with my foot, just a few times so that it wasn't underfoot.

I lifted my foot up, and hoped to god it was still there, nearly sighing with relief when my hand clasped around that handle. How my knife had stayed lodged in my boot without cutting half of my foot off I had no idea, but it was there alright, and I clasped hold of it as tight as I could, pulled it slowly out, and took a deep breath.

I nearly hesitated, nearly couldn't do it, but then from far back in the darkness, probably in some dingy corridor of the warehouse that I hadn't seen, came a muffled scream. No one around me even took any notice of it, but it was clear to me, and it sounded like a child's scream.

I rammed the knife as hard as I could up into Eddie's belly. No hesitation now, just hatred and pure violent instinct.

The shock hit me as the knife disappeared nearly up to the hilt. Six inches of wicked, serrated blade vanished into him, just like he was made of butter, and it was just as easy coming out as it was going in. I pulled hard and nearly let go of the knife as it whipped back out again.

The noise Eddie made, as he let go of the scruff of my neck and keeled over to the ground in front of me, was also nothing like I imagined it would be. I had heard a scream before, but never the scream of a dying man whose belly was spilling out over the floor in front of him. I hadn't realised it, but as I pulled the blade out, Eddie must have felt the pain and pulled away, turning at the same time. His panicked struggle to escape the pain opened up his belly almost from hip to hip. All those years of over indulgence came spilling out in front of him with a wet slosh and a thud. I have no idea which bit of his insides made that horrible noise as it hit the floor, but whatever it was, it hit the wooden board so hard that it ruptured. Blood and a nasty green and yellow gunk splattered everywhere.

I didn't stay around to see what happened next,

though as I ran into the dark, trying to find a way to escape this awful place, I heard screams, mostly Eddie's I believe, and shouts, and even laughter. I was pretty sure that at least a dozen folks standing nearby got covered with Eddie's guts and they were probably freaking out about now, but I wasn't staying around long enough to find out.

I stumbled into the darkness, running blind, turning corner after corner and darting around people. I was sure I went the same way several times in my blundering attempt at an escape. I could feel hands reach out at me, and shouts called. Some were probably just in surprise, but others were to alert anyone trying to catch me. I couldn't find a back door, and was panicking. I remembered that there were guards there who might stop me anyway, so I ran for the next nearest exit I could find, which was out through an open archway and onto the walkway that ran along the side of the river. I had to jump over a figure sitting in the doorway, huddled up and dressed in rags. Fortunately whoever that was either didn't notice or didn't care.

As the shouts followed me outside, getting closer, I ran along the thin strip of cobbled ground at the back of the building, looking for a way out. I could see that the walkway ended in a sheer wall, and my heart nearly jumped into my throat as I turned around and saw three angry-looking men, one of them Remy, jogging towards me barely twenty feet away.

There was no way out, I thought, but then I saw it, the wall that ran alongside the walkway, separating it from the river, carried on further, a small foot wide gap that carried on past the sheer wall at the end, one that a boy might run along, but a man would struggle with. I ran again, just as I heard a clicking noise and saw at the edge of my vision that Remy had lifted the gun that he had taken from Mr Holcroft's workshop. I took a hopeful leap onto the wall, but lost my footing, tripped, and banged my knee. I reached out, but not fast enough, and toppled over the wall, falling into those dark waters.

The pain of the cold water hit me as I plunged into the flowing stream. I gasped for breath, my arms flailing as I struggled to pull myself up. Just as I thought it was all over, I managed to put my head above the water, and fill my lungs with air. There was a loud bang, and the water just a few feet away splashed. Something unseen whizzed past my face. I looked back towards the warehouse to see Remy trying to reload the gun, but he gave up as I drifted away, pulled by the strong current, down the Thames river and out into the city.

I never saw Remy again, but I would remember the curses he yelled at me that night.

I would remember those my whole life.

For the first time, I was truly alone. As I emerged from the river in another area of the city, utterly frightened, cold and wet, I remember wondering if Eddie was okay. I was only young, and it took a while for me to realise what I had done. Eddie was not okay, and never would be again.

Before I was even eight years old, I had killed a man. It wouldn't be the last time, there were many more to follow in my life, but it was certainly the one that haunts me the most.

# 3

The pain today is especially sharp. The doctor came this morning to visit, and he said that I would get periods of time where it would be painful, and others where I might think I was perfectly fine. It makes me wonder where they get all this from. He can't be any older than maybe thirty years old. What would he know about pain? Don't get me wrong, he has probably seen a whole lot of people suffering, but to know what real pain is like?

You know there are some things that I believe are worse than physical pain, loneliness for one of them. I spent a long time wandering London after I escaped from the warehouse that night, and a lot of nights alone in the dark, sleeping under bridges and down alleyways, watching people go by, wondering who they were and where they might be going.

I often wondered during those days whether anyone thought that of me as they wandered by. Not that they would always see me. I did my utmost to keep out of sight, keep to the shadows and disappear whenever someone came by, but that didn't always work.

It was rare during those days to meet anyone who cared much about anyone else. Everyone was far too busy suffering in their own way in that overcrowded and run-down city. Yeah, it had its beauty too, but when you walk a few streets along and turn a corner, you start to see the uglier side, the side that most normal folks wouldn't even have known was just a short distance away.

But, saying all that, I did occasionally meet some good folks, just like the folks of a place that I would never forget.

The Running Ground.

My stay there was much shorter than I would have liked, but the folks there, and the community of it all, have stayed with me my whole life.

There are some things you don't ever forget.

The Running Ground was a patch of land that ran between the arches of the railway and a shoe factory, just a dozen acres of overgrown ruins that had once been a street. Running through the middle of it was what I imagined had once been a cobbled road with pavement on either side, but that was all broken up and overgrown with weeds now. Rows of what once had been buildings played house to the teeming homeless. Immigrants, the old, the disabled, and plenty of people just down on their luck.

It was a pretty ugly place to live, but it was where I called home, for a while. After what must have been months of wandering London alone, it was good to see at least a few friendly faces.

I'd spent most of my nights since that night at the warehouse, living under bridges or huddled in some dark corner in a derelict building. My days were spent scavenging what I could find to live on, scraps and dustbin leftovers mostly. Yes, there were restaurants and markets to scrounge something from, but unless you were living on those streets back then you couldn't know just how many people were in the same situation. London was heaving with the homeless and the destitute.

One day I had decided to move on, move to a different area. I'd been stealing from the same few dozen shops and market stalls for months, and the owners could spot me coming.

It was by accident that I found the Running Ground. It was late at night and I was trying to find somewhere to hide away from the rain. It was beating down with a vengeance and had been for three days. My clothes were soaked all the way to my skin, and the cold bit me all the way to my bones. I snuck into a rundown building through one of the bottom windows that had been smashed, and when I realised the place was unoccupied I made my way up the stairs to one of the back rooms. I'd sat under an archway in the alley directly across from the house for at least an hour, just trying to spy out whether anyone was in there. I'd seen nothing. I also hadn't seen the rooms downstairs, all stacked high with boxes and wooden cases.

Before I lay down to try and sleep I looked out of the back window. There, sprawled as far as I could see, was the shanty town that was the Running

Ground. From my view up in the window it looked like a maze of huts and junk. In between the huts, dotted here and there, underneath the tall brick archways of the railway, were fires burning in old barrels, or roughly built brick circles. The homeless folks gathered around them in their droves.

The old man had risked his own neck just coming in after me, though I guessed he was much more used to moving around unnoticed than I was, because I didn't even hear him coming up the stairs. How he had seen me, I will never know.

"Boy," he said, though it sounded more like a dog's bark.

I spun round. My heart was pounding.

"Out, quickly. You can't be in here."

He turned and moved back towards the top of the stairs, glancing back at me several times with an irritated look.

"Don't just stand there gawping at me boy. If they find you in here it will be Breaker's Alley for you."

I didn't know what Breaker's Alley was, and by that name I wasn't sure I wanted to either. I gathered my few things and rushed down the stairs after him.

We went out the back door and climbed over the wall. From the window upstairs it had looked small, but it rose at least seven feet tall at the very back, and there was no back gate. Fortunately there was a small stone shed that was part collapsed. I copied the old man and jumped up on it, shimmied to the back wall, and hauled myself over.

Hands grabbed me out of the darkness, and pulled me through tall grass and thorns. I tried to cry out, but someone clamped their hand over my mouth. It wasn't the old man.

They let me go once they had dragged me through a gap in the huts and hauled me into a half stone, half wooden shed. I looked around at my captors. Two old men and a young woman, maybe in her late twenties, all dressed in layer upon layer of dirty rags and scrap clothing.

I pulled my legs in close, ready to run if I had to.

"Are you trying to get yourself killed, young man?"

It was the woman who spoke. Her voice was soft, warm even, and the look she gave me reminded me more of a cross but amused mother than a stranger.

"No. I'm sorry." I wasn't sure what I was making excuses for.

"That building," she said, pointing behind me, "is a safe house for contraband, owned by The Breakers." She looked at me like she was expecting me to react in some way, like I should have known what she was talking about.

"I'm sorry. I didn't know," I replied, lowering my head. At the same time I was looking for the nearest exit.

"No point saying sorry to us," she continued. "It's not us that will kill you if you're found in there."

A door opened in the darkness opposite me, spewing in the light from one of the many fires that I had seen out of the window. The old man who had hurried me out of the house stepped inside the shed to join us, nodding to the others.

"All clear," he said. "No one about."

The woman turned back to me.

"You are very lucky, child. Now go," she said, indicating the still open door.

As I got up and headed towards the door, still nervous of the people around me, she called out.

"There is food over the way. Look for the big man with a huge beard over near the arches. Don't worry, he is friendly enough."

So it was that I stepped out into the main street of The Running Ground for the first time, and to say that place changed my life would be an understatement. Ever since my narrow escape at The Warehouse I had been living day to day, struggling just to find something to eat. But here, amongst some of the strangest and most destitute folks I'd ever met, was a haven of sorts.

There must have been a thousand people living in that slum when I arrived. To this day I don't know how long it had been there, but I heard one old tramp say once that he had been one of the first, and that had been before the turn of the century, before I was born. Huddled in makeshift huts, some of them even two or three stories high, were people from all over, and every walk of life. Don't even ask how those things stayed standing.

It didn't take me long to find the food. I just followed the smell of cooking.

The Chef, as they called him, was an Indian man, and he was one of the tallest men I have ever seen in my life. I think he was seven feet tall at the least, probably taller. I never did learn his real name, only that he had come to England with his parents when he was a child, brought by a family who owned a lot of land in his home country. His parents had died when he was even younger than I was.

He took one look at me and filled a metal bowl full of some hot stew from the barrel that he was cooking it in, tore off a chunk of dry, stale bread from a box next to it and handed it to me, pointing at a bench nearby where some other children were sitting, eating. I didn't ask what the stew was, didn't much care. It was hot and it filled me up. The bread was like eating a rock, but I didn't complain. I was so hungry, and no one bothered me as I sat there, quietly stuffing my face as fast as I could.

When I finished the stew I took the plate back over to The Chef and asked him where I cleaned them. He just smiled, took the bowl, filled it up a second time, and handed it back to me. I must have looked quite comical standing there with my jaw nearly bouncing off the floor, because he just laughed.

"When your done, you wash in the barrel," he said, in between his laughter. He pointed at another barrel that was propped up against the arch wall a few feet away.

There were a lot of strange folk living on The Running Ground, but amongst them were a lot of good people too. Apart from the odd few, most of them stuck together, sharing everything they got their hands on, which was mostly scavenged from bins, run-down houses, or scrap yards.

It turned out that most of the food that kept everybody alive was stolen from all over London, or pulled out of market bins. There were a lot of mouths to feed, and anyone who was good at taking stuff without been seen soon found themselves pretty high up the pecking order.

I fitted in almost immediately. I was small, quiet, and fast. Within a week I was friendly with a lot of the folks who lived in that dingy slum. All I wanted most of the time was a full belly and some place to sleep. The first I could do myself, but somewhere safe to sleep meant I had to get things for other people.

It was easy enough to grab something when the owner of a market stall or a shop wasn't looking, but soon they would start to wondert why you were hanging around, and most of them had been robbed enough times by street rats like me that they just sent you on your way even before you got near. I learned to do things a different way.

There were some busy streets in London, and if you were small you could disappear into the crowd and be barely noticed, so long as you didn't stink too badly. That certainly made a difference. So here is what I would do. Once in amongst the crowd you just start walking along, up and down the street, changing direction every now and then to stay with the flow of folks, and you would keep your hands busy. Into this pocket there, or this bag over here. Most of the time those pockets would be empty, or you would put your hand into a bag and come out with nothing useful, but if you carried on, eventually you would swipe something good. I had watches, purses, lockets, a whole lot of keys, jewellery. The list was endless.

I was an extraordinary pickpocket.

Did I ever get caught? Well of course I did, but if you are fast, like I was, you just kept walking when the shout went up, and you dropped whatever it was that you had just taken. You never, ever, ever kept everything you had taken that day on you. Oh no, because when you got caught you had to be carrying nothing, and of course you had just dropped whatever it was that you took, so when folks started looking around, it usually turned up and whoever was shouting about thieves looked stupid themselves.

I used to stash my finds somewhere nearby, somewhere out of the way and hidden, like a hole between some bricks, in an alleyway, anywhere that wasn't going to be disturbed, that I could go to without being watched.

There were at least a dozen shops hidden away in back streets that would take whatever you stole and hand you a few coins. I knew every time I sold something that It was worth a lot more than what I had just been given, but it didn't matter, those few coins bought me the food from the shops that I might have stolen from at one time.

I never sold my knife.

It was always tucked into its little holder, hanging off my belt under my jacket.

I used to keep hold of some of my "finds" and take them back as gifts to folks I liked on the Running Ground, or I'd hand out a few coins. That bought me a bed in nearly every shack in the place, but mostly I slept at the back of Chef's place.

One very hot day in 1912, about four years after I first started living at the Running Ground, some policemen came by. They were looking for someone, someone who it seemed had been poking around in the buildings that ran along near the street, like the one that I had snuck into to sleep in.

They roughed up a few people, and even gave Chef some grief, but in truth, nobody knew who it had been. One of the old boys said he had seen a bunch of young men, street folk, hanging around the front a week or so before, said they hadn't been back since. He gave the policemen a description of them as best he could, before they beat the crap out of him anyway, and threatened him with the Breaker's Alley. Then they went on their way.

I never did like the police, at least not those ones. I'm sure that lots of policemen were doing their job and were good people, but those ones, they were as bad a bunch of men as could be. Evil I would say.

After they had gone I sat near the old boy they had harassed.

"What did that man mean by the Breaker's Alley?" I asked.

He turned and frowned at me, like I was intruding somewhere I shouldn't have been, but then his expression softened.

"It's just what they call it," he said, "though that isn't the name on the street sign."

"Then why do they call it that if it's not the name of the street?" I asked.

He just looked at me solemnly and told me that it was where people got broken.

"What do you mean they get broken?" I asked.

"Just trust me son, you don't want to find yourself in the Breaker's Alley at the wrong time. Don't want to find yourself in there at any time really. Some things are best not seen."

"So what's the street really called?" I asked.

"Hemley, I think," he said, "Hemley Alley."

"Strange name for a street." I said.

"Tis indeed," said the old man, with a half-hearted smile.

I was going to ask more, but I could tell that I was irritating him. The policemen had scared him, scared them all pretty badly, and I thought he just wanted to be left alone to his whiskey.

About two weeks after that I discovered for myself what the Breaker's Alley was. I didn't mean to, and I never ended up there on purpose.

As I said before, I was a great pickpocket, and it hadn't gone unnoticed amongst the Running Ground folks. Unfortunately, it seemed that the same bunch of thugs that had broken into the store houses and stolen from the Breakers had also spotted me going into a pawn shop, just down the street. I would guess that they had been watching me as well, without me noticing them until it was too late.

I was making my way home when they jumped me. I left the same shop one evening, just as it was getting dark, and turned into the alleyway at the back.

There were five of them, none of them as fast as me, but they were strong, and they had me surrounded.

"What you got there lad?" said one of them. He was shorter than the rest, and had a mouth full of missing or rotten teeth. He smiled at me and I could tell there was no friendliness in that smile.

"Nothing," I said, trying to judge the gaps between them, see if I could make a run for it.

"Oh, I don't think you've got nothing," he said, "I think you've got a pocket there full of coins, and I think you're going to hand it to me."

He stepped forward and grabbed me by the

shoulder, pushing me against a wall, pinning me. He went through my pockets but couldn't find anything. He stopped smiling at me, and didn't notice as my hand slipped to my belt, my knife out of its holder.

"Where are they son?" he asked, through gritted teeth. "You best hand them over now or I'm going to smash you up."

He reached forward again, grabbing me by both shoulders and pushing hard.

It was only the second time I had used the knife. I'd taken it out a couple of times since that night at The Warehouse, but I'd never actually had to use it on anyone since then. I don't think he even noticed the blade jab up into his arm, not for a few seconds. It was as far as I could reach with my shoulders pinned. Then he started screaming, and blood was pouring out of his arm and going everywhere. He let go of me and stumbled back, just enough for me to dart by him and run for the gap between two of his thugs. The first of them was too distracted by all the blood spurting out of RottenTooth's arm, but the second one made a grab for me. One hand shot out towards me and snatched the back of my jacket. It didn't stop me running. I lashed out at his hand, and then just kept on going, glancing back quickly as he also started screaming.

I'd cut off four of the fingers on his hand.

I ran and ran, as fast as I could, through alleyways that I thought would lead me to the Running Ground, and they followed me, I could hear them not far behind me, and I could hear the bellowing yells. I was normally good at disappearing into these alleyways, but somehow I just couldn't shake them. They knew this place as well as I did.

Then I turned a corner, and ran headlong into two men blocking the way. They grabbed me and threw me to the floor. I hit the ground hard, stunned, opened my eyes and looked down the alleyway. Behind me I could hear RottenTooth's gang come round the corner and soon there was shouting, but I wasn't paying attention to that. It was nothing to the horror that I saw before me.

There were at least a dozen men in the alleyway, most of them moving past me quickly, joining in the fight that was going on behind me. Just a few feet away, was a body. I didn't recognise her, but I knew by the way she was dressed that she was a street prostitute, now lying dead in a pool of blood that was gradually spreading. Behind her was just one man who was holding onto a girl I recognised.

She was tied up and gagged, but I could still see her eyes. It was the girl from The Warehouse, the one who I had dreamed about for so many nights after.

Next to the man was another prostitute, and she was standing against the wall holding her head. I could see she was bleeding from a cut over her eye.

She was looking around, dazed, but then something happened, I think maybe she got her senses back for a moment, and saw that only one man was between her and escape. She launched herself at him, kicking him and punching him. The girl fell over as the man struggled with both of them, but then he reached to his waist and pulled out a gun.

The noise was so loud that it left my ears ringing, but I knew I didn't have time to wait. I had to react now.

I ran forward, my knife still in my hand. The prostitute hadn't even hit the ground when I rushed forward and stuck the blade straight into the man's throat. I don't think he even saw me coming.

I stumbled as he fell backwards, dropping his gun and hitting the ground, gargling. I hissed at the girl to run. She was gagged and tied by the hands, but her feet were still free, so we took off up that alleyway as fast as we could, only stopping when neither of us could run another yard. We collapsed in the doorway of a boarded-up building. I had no idea where we were, but it was dark and there was no one around.

I helped her take the gag off, and removed the ropes from her hands. We sat there, breathing heavily, both too shocked to say a word.

"I'm Reg," I said, when I finally got my breath back.

"I'm Marie," she said, looking at me through those huge, stunning, frightened eyes.

She was the same age as me except for a couple of days. She told me all about how she had been bought by the owner of a brothel in London's East End. She was still too young to ply that trade, and had not been the most cooperative girl that the owner had bought from The Warehouse. Fortunately the man's wife had taken a shine to her, and set her to work in the kitchen and the wash room. The owner, a man called Norton, had insisted that there were customers that would have paid a lot of money to spend time with Marie, but his wife had insisted and he eventually gave in.

That night she had been heading over to the brothel, taking some clean sheets and clothes over for some of the girls, when the Breakers had caught them.

"They were going to kill us," she said, "and I don't know why."

Marie knew the name of the town just outside of London that she had come from, even gave me a detailed account of how she had been snatched one day. It was a place called Gravesend. I said I had to go back to the Running Ground and tell Chef what had happened, but then I would help her get home.

Chef listened quietly while I told him all about what had happened, everything from how I'd got caught by RottenTooth and then ran into the Breakers by accident.

"You hide up here, and stay quiet," he said, and then went off to have a word around, to find out what was happening.

He came back about an hour later and told me to get my things together fast. It seemed that one of the Breakers had recognised me, and now they were looking for me and Marie.

"You have to go," he said. "The man you stabbed, well, he is dead, and he was their leader, and they are out for blood. They will find you if they come here, and kill you both. They are looking now, and it will not be long before they come here. "

"But they'll hurt folks when they come here." I said.

Chef smiled and ruffled my hair.

"You don't worry too much about us. You get yourself away now."

I bit back the tears as I quickly said my goodbyes to folks. Then Chef walked us to the edge of the Running Ground and shook my hand as he said goodbye.

"We will see each other again Reggie boy, we will. I have a good feeling about that," he said, hugging me so hard I could barely breathe.

"I hope so," I replied.

It took us a week to get to Gravesend. Not that it was far, but neither of us knew how to get there and I was too wary to ask anyone we passed for directions, just in case the Breakers were somehow trailing us. The last thing I wanted was to get Marie back home, only to have them turn up.

It was a week that I will always remember fondly. We spent most of our days travelling around the south of London, looking for street signs that might help us. At night we would sometimes find an abandoned building and break in, other times we just slept under a bridge or in a dark corner in some alleyway. Two young kids wrapped up in rags could disappear quite easily in all the litter and junk that was piled up in the alleyways.

It was a beautiful sunny day when we eventually walked into Gravesend and found the street that Marie used to live on. Along the street, right outside the house that she had lived in was the same horse-drawn cart that her father had owned back when she was taken.

We stood holding each other tight for a long while before I eventually pulled away and told her to go. It was nice that she was reluctant to do so, but I could see that her eyes were sparkling with joy as she said goodbye and ran up the street.

"I won't forget you ever, Reggie," she said, before she ran to the house.

"I won't forget you either," I said quietly. I don't think she heard me.

She stopped at the gate and looked back, waved, and ran to the front door. A moment later and I heard cries of joy coming from inside the house. I smiled, turned away, and started walking back towards London.

I never did tell her what I saw a few nights before we said goodbye, as we huddled together in a doorway on a particularly cold night.

It was bitter cold. The wind was howling down

the alleyway, and the best that we could do was to huddle close together in the doorway of the run down building. I looked through one of the windows, hoping that it might be a good place to break in and sleep for the night, but I saw rats. Marie was so tired that we couldn't keep looking.

She fell asleep, leaning on my shoulder, after just a few minutes, but I was wide awake, I just couldn't seem to drop off. We were hidden well enough behind the bins that were propped up in front of the doorway, so the chances of anyone finding us were quite small, but that wasn't enough for me. I only felt safe if we were tucked away in the dark, at the back of a room in a building.

I think it was about an hour after Marie fell asleep that I saw them, and I would say that there were a dozen of them at least. Dark figures, dressed in robes of some kind. They didn't look like they were even walking along the alleyway. They just kind of drifted along. I couldn't see their feet underneath all those long robes.

My hackles went up immediately, and I instinctively put my hand down to my knife, still tucked in its holder at my waist, but they either hadn't noticed us, or they chose to ignore us.

Until the last one passed us by.

She walked by at least a few feet, and then stopped, turned slowly around to face us, and pulled the hood off.

It was one of the dead prostitutes, the ones who

had been killed in that alleyway. Except she wasn't dead anymore, no way, she was standing there as alive as she had been just before the man with the gun shot her in the head.

I didn't know what to do. The others stopped as well, some of them just standing still, some turning to face us. It was then that I realised that there was something very different about them, something that sent a chill to my bones.

Their skin was as pale as a dead man, eyes as dark as night, and not one of them had any white to their eyes, just an endless darkness, like shiny black orbs, glowing fiercely in the moonlight.

The dead prostitute looked at me, and then she looked at Marie, who was still fast asleep on my shoulder, then she smiled, and I saw something else that had changed.

Fangs.

That's right. She had what I can best describe as fangs. Two long and pointed incisors that had no place in a human mouth, at least not naturally.

I thought we were about to die, but I was wrong. She simply nodded in Marie's direction, smiled at me again, turned and carried on walking off.

The rest of the group continued on their way, leaving me with my heart beating like it was about to explode, and Marie still sleeping on my shoulder.

That was what I never told her about.

I really wish that I had.

# 4

I've often asked myself, why didn't I just stay in Gravesend? Why didn't I just stick around there for a while? I sure would have liked to have spent more time with Marie, but you know, I was a dirty street boy, and once she was all cleaned up and healthy again, well, I don't think her folks would have been keen on her hanging around with my type, if you know what I mean.

There was also something about Gravesend that didn't fit with me. I did take a wander around there before I walked back to London, and I decided that there just weren't enough places for me to hide.

Today a gentleman named Alexander Winters has come to join me in the hospital. He isn't as old as I am, but I like to think he looks older. Seems he may not be a permanent resident though, and has been through most of what I have been through already, except he appears to be on the road to recovery. He used to be a cobbler, or at least that's what he says. I don't know what they call shoe workers these days. Probably something like a Footwear Operative or a Leisurewear Executive or something like that. They do seem to like their names these days, don't they?

He is a genial enough old boy, likes to talk a lot, which is good, since I don't. I think I'm getting used to this Dictaphone though.

It's good that it doesn't answer me back.

That name.

Winters.

That takes me back a long, long time. I had a friend with exactly the same last name once, though he was a much bigger man. I keep meaning to ask if Alexander might be related to him, but when the moment comes I don't know how to put it into words. Such a long time ago to remember some of these things, yet they all seem to me like they happened only yesterday.

After I left Gravesend, and Marie behind me, I headed straight back into London, though not back to The Running Ground, no, I could never go back there again, not unless I wanted to get myself, and maybe others, killed.

For the next couple of years, I wandered London. Sometimes I found myself a home in one of the workshops or the hovels that spread across the city during those days, and other times I ended up back on the streets and homeless again, spending my time hanging around on street corners amongst the throng of other folks left useless and hungry. Those were the worst times, scraping to make it by, to even find enough food to eat. But there were ways to survive in a city that big, if you knew where to look and you weren't too fussy about what you had to do to get there.

My life through those years was not pleasant by any means, but I have nothing to tell you about that time that is much different to anybody else who was alone and frightened in London during the early years of the twentieth century. That isn't what I need to talk about at all.

Throughout most of my years I was haunted by a face, a vision that I saw in the early years of the First World War. It took a long time for that face to disappear from my nightmares, which it did eventually, but it has never completely left me.

When I was fifteen years old I was caught stealing in Soho, London, it was just a few things to eat, and a newspaper for a man who I had been doing some labour work for. Doesn't sound like a lot, but my face was remembered around those parts for committing similar offences the year before. I was locked up in a cell and told that I was to face a trial soon, when they got round to it.

Of course we were part-way through the war at that time, and while I was waiting to attend my trial, a man in a uniform showed up at the prison, checking each of the cells in turn. I remember his face very well, He was tall, and healthy looking, but there was something in his eyes that said he was tired, tired of living and tired of the worries. He had a large brown moustache, and was wearing a long army coat. I had seen many of those coats in London over the last few years, but very rarely saw the same faces twice.

He looked down at me as I sat on that cell bed, glanced at the prison warden who was accompanying him, and nodded.

"He'll do," he said, and then moved on to the next cell, where Larry Raymuss had committed suicide the night before, and lay cold and dead on his bunk, still waiting for somebody to come along and discover him. Poor Larry had problems of a mental kind, he was what they called "touched" and had cried himself to sleep nearly every night, mumbling constantly and incoherently, before he finally silenced himself.

When they discovered Larry he was drained of every drop of blood in his body, after cutting his wrists on the jagged metal edge of his bunk. That might not sound so strange, and it wasn't uncommon to see folks end their lives deliberately in the cells, except there was very little blood on the floor or on his bed. No, Larry had cut his wrists and painstakingly written, for everybody to see, the sins of his life, across the walls and the ceiling, even under the window, in his own blood, line after line of detailed accounts of the crimes he had committed, and of those that had been committed against him. I never saw it myself. I only heard the warden and the guards shouting about it as I lay on my bunk, quietly contemplating what was to become of me.

That Larry wrote what he did was an amazing feat in itself, but what was more worrying wasn't the details of the crimes, it was the other stuff, the unreadable stuff. For written in among his confession Larry had scrawled some strange script that no one could recognise. Not even the language professor from the big university that they called in could make any of it out.

That professor clearly didn't want to be down there in those cells with all the scum of London. I could see through the bars of my cells just enough to make out his face as he looked into Larry's room. He stood there for a minute or so just staring in horror at the room. Then he tried to read it all, not just the stuff written in English, but the other writings. He said something about it looking archaic, or something along those lines, but he swore he couldn't decipher it.

The prison warden didn't look convinced, but eventually he let it go, and let the professor go. That man scrambled out of the prison faster than a dog chasing a rabbit, nearly tripping over his own feet as he bolted up the stairs. I wouldn't be surprised if that man never answered to a similar call in his life after that.

And do you know what else I think, I think that those mumblings that Larry made during the night, that incomprehensible chatter, I'm damn sure that was what he wrote, and to someone it would have made sense, though I would never have wanted to meet that particular someone, not at all.

My military visitor had signed over my fate to the war, or so it seemed for me and for a number of other prisoners in that block. We were marched out to the yard and told that we would be leaving that afternoon.

I was much younger than the draft age, but sometime during my stay in the cells someone had changed my age on a document to say I was five years older. They showed me the papers, smiling wickedly as I fumbled through them. They must have presumed that I couldn't read, and of course I could. There on the page was a scribble mark and the new number '21' under the age of offender.

Now I don't know if that military gentleman believed it when he saw me, but he must have had some reason to decide I was to go, because he glanced at me for a moment, with an almost knowing look, said his few words that sent me out of that block and into a whole other world of chaos, and then moved on to the next cell, not even looking back, and I don't think he once considered what he had just signed me over to. He probably hadn't a clue himself.

Why did he let a young boy, years from a drinking age, go to probably die in the trenches? I don't know. I don't suppose I'll ever know the answer to that question.

So at the age of only fifteen I was shipped off to a training camp, where at least I got fed properly for a few weeks. From there it was onto a boat across the Channel. I had never been on the sea, and I spent the first half an hour marvelling at the view of the ocean, and then most of the remaining trip hurling my guts up over the edge. By the time I stopped being sick, we were near the coast of a whole other country.

We travelled across France for many miles, and you know, apart from the dirt and stench of war, it wasn't that much different to being in the country back home. Okay, the war had torn apart some of what might once have been civilisation, there were ruined buildings all over, but the odd time we crossed a place that hadn't seen fighting for a while, I might as well have been back home.

But eventually I found myself hunkered down in a trench, dodging bullets, and dreading the moment we would have to go over the top.

One day in June there was a major offensive, a push that we were told could change the war. I think it was just a pep talk that they tried to give us, with a genuine expression on their faces, before they told us we were to climb up and head over the killing ground to die. That day was the last for many of the men I had grown to know, and many more I would never have the chance to speak to. It was the day of the gas attacks, and also the day that the world ended for thousands of men. For the very first time I began to suspect that everything you see in life is not always clear.

I had made friends with a couple of the older soldiers in the months that I fought in those trenches. There was old Looky, an aged man who had been the army for most of his life, and he loved to smoke his pipe when he could get some tobacco.

There was also Winters, another older soldier who it seemed had taken a shine to me early on. He was from the north of England, and at the start I found it hard to understand him, but I got used to his strong Yorkshire accent eventually.

The three of us stuck together, which often meant I tagged along behind, following them for guidance. Both of those old guys had been in the war from the beginning, and Looky had been over the top at least a dozen times. He said it was all about luck, but I knew otherwise. Those two old soldiers had a way about them, call it a karma - they just kept on going, and fate followed them every step of the way. There was something they were meant for, I guess something like what I think I was meant for, to witness, to be there when something happened, and to be there to take notice. After my experience in that slave shop in London all those years ago, seeing those faces that came back to haunt me every night when I slept, I think I was ready when it finally happened, when the next strangeness reared up and waved its hand at me.

I had been over the top only once, and it was a very short distance into a trench that was barely defended. Don't get me wrong, I had my share of near misses just being there, but the one time we had been given the order to move, we met very little resistance. So when we moved on the hill that afternoon I was little prepared for what I was to see.

Across from where we had found our little hole to bed down in for the few weeks that we held the trench at the bottom of the hill, was a stretch of land that had seen a lot of fighting in the months prior to my arrival. Winters told me that nearly a whole battalion had been lost in those few hundred yards. I occasionally took a moment to spy out across that stretch of land, much to the annoyance of my new guardians. But being young and stupid, I had to look. Morbid curiosity is a natural human trait that I had accepted a long time ago, it's never been a thing I denied. Everybody has it. I think that it's part of our make-up.

The nearest and most visible one sat bolt upright barely twenty yards across the run. He was leaning against a twisted, splintered stump that might once have been the most majestic of trees. It was nearly ten feet across, and perched on our side of the stump was Harold. I don't know why I named him that, but it was soon taken on by everyone in our trench. Old Harold sat there with his shoulders proud and his rifle leaning against the stump, still held firmly in his hands. What he was missing was his head. He could have been anybody, looked like anybody and come from any place in the world and you wouldn't have known.

He was the first marker, the guideline for where death started. Up on that hill they were so bedded down that not even the artillery had managed to make much of a dent.

The guns had been sounding for three days almost constantly, a never-ending din of deep, ground-shaking thuds as they sent their payload roaring up into the sky to come crashing down on the entrenchments that circled again and again. Each time a bombardment finished we waited, and waited, and each time our enemies took to their mud walls again and answered with their own guns.

They didn't have any of the massive artillery emplacements that sat behind us, but what they did have was enough to shower the ground between the lines with a deadly thunder.

We would duck down to avoid any fragments from the assault, and be glad that our trenches were just that bit too far for them to reach. Old Harold would sit through all of it, somehow managing to stay upright and proud, while the land around him erupted in a deluge of fire and mud. I think if he hadn't lost his head, his chin would have been raised to the skies in defiance.

When the call went up that last time, before we took to the killing ground to make our assault, I somehow knew it was coming. There was a chill in the air. Fog had descended over the fields, and the top of the hill was masked from sight. At that moment following the shrill pierce of the whistles that signalled our time to advance, just on the edge of visibility I saw for the first time that Old Harold had moved. No longer did he hold his weapon upright, and no longer was his back straight against the rock. He had slumped forward as if finally giving in.

So it was that on that cold afternoon, with the sun blocked by mist and the skies grey, the guns went silent one last time.

We poured out of those trenches like ants stumbling out into the light to face some unknown giant. Winters was the first over the top, followed quickly by Looky. I fumbled to climb the broken ladder, and I was easily ten feet behind them when I finally leapt over the escarpment and began running to catch up with them. I glanced to my side and it seemed we were the fastest out of the trench, but within seconds the killing ground was a mass of bodies rushing for the slope of the hill. Four hundred yards away, past the slumped body of Old Harold, through an abandoned trench, the barbed wire twisted and torn from the constant pounding it had received from both sides, and over a stretch of ground that was pock marked with craters, mud and body parts. That was where we had to reach. The bottom of the hill and the cover that it would give us.

The trench was surprisingly easy to cross. That barbed wire was so damaged that I didn't even slow down when I reached it, I followed Winters and Looky's example and just leapt up, out and down into the drop, landing heavily. One foot sank deep into the mud, missing the rocks that Winters and Looky had used with such agility to reach the other side. The other foot crunched straight down on the head of a dead soldier, one of ours by the looks of it. I saw his pale wide-eyed face for a moment before my weight sank the only part of him that wasn't already submerged into the mud.

It was just as I reached the top of the trench and started running out across the open ground, that the silence ended.

The hilltop guns unleashed their fury down upon us.

They were firing blind, but I was pretty sure that they had heard the whistles that signalled the assault, because the guns spoke heavier than they had from the trenches. Maybe it was just my imagination, and my being in the middle of the killing ground when the bullets started to hit.

Winters and Looky were easily ten yards ahead of me now, and all I could do as the whistling sound of deadly fire began to flash by my ears was put my head down and charge like a bull across the ground, hoping that I could make it to the other side. Behind me, I heard the telling sounds of the carnage that was to come as the first screams of men began to sound in their hundreds across the length of our trench lines.

I think I was lucky, although I was sure I felt bullets brush by me, and I know one missed my shoulder by barely an inch, leaving a dark scorch mark on my jacket. I think that I had cleared most of the ground that they were firing upon by the time they started shooting. There were a few explosions not far from me as I ran, and I was vaguely aware of others running across the same ground, but that open ground, towards the cover of the hill where Looky and Winters were crouched, waiting, was too quiet, too still. Apart from the guns roaring above us and the screams of the dying behind me, no one on that field made a sound.

My shoulder wrenched with pain as I hit the stone ramparts at the bottom of the hill. My friends were ten yards further along the wall to my right, I guess I had lost track of them and veered off as an explosion sounded a few feet behind me. The mud was deep and I struggled to crawl through it to reach them, suddenly aware that I was covered in blood, though I felt no pain, so it couldn't have been my own. Then I noticed what it was I was crawling on.

Half buried in the mud at the bottom of the hill were bodies, hundreds of them, rotten and plump, full of maggots, and they weren't whole either, many of them were just bits of body, Legs and arms, torsos and heads all submerged in the slush that lay next to the wall. The uniforms weren't the same colour as ours, so I guess our hilltop nemesis had found a way to get rid of their dead, to stop them from stinking up the place, and we had the misfortune to have to sit in amongst it. Behind me someone called out in disgust, and I spun round to see a young man crawling back away from the wall, horror in his eyes as he looked down upon the open cavity of a ribcage into which a head had fallen, neatly, smiling its rotten grin out at us.

I tried to call out to him as he backed away from the wall, but my voice had gone, and all that came out was a harsh rasp. I was too late anyway. Gunfire exploded from the hill above and his body erupted and fell apart, pieces flying across the ground away from the wall. Two other men running towards the hill were caught in the gun's arc, as it spread outward from its target and into the oncoming throng of desperate men, all so close to the temporary safety that the rampart offered, they too were torn apart.

It was the last time I heard the guns from above. One minute they were thundering down upon us, and the next, they fell silent.

It took us a while to crawl around the side of the hill to a small break in the rampart that Winters had spotted. There, the wall opened up into the first layer of trenches, blown apart by artillery shells. The hole must have been fresh, because as the three of us stumbled forward into the trench we were greeted by the remains of our enemies. Only one man was still alive, dragging himself slowly up the slope of the trench, his legs detached at the knees. He was blabbering and yelling something unrecognisable for a moment, before Winters picked up the man's own rifle and put a bullet in the back of his head.

I don't know what I had expected as we made our way through the winding paths of the hilltop fort. I know that I didn't expect it to be so empty of the living. We crawled and picked our way through three layers of trenches before we found anyone alive. And that single man was sitting shivering and talking the same nonsense as the legless guys down below, his machine gun hanging useless from its wall placement where he had abandoned it. He saw us, and ran straight for the sandbags, jumping out into open space to fall head first to the ground below.

Through all the trenches we found endless piles of the dead, but none of them seemed injured. There were no bullet wounds or half-blown-up defenders, just bodies lying in the dirt. Winters checked a few of them as we went, and confirmed that they were dead, but all the same he couldn't find a reason why.

The three of us finally raised the British flag high on the top of the hill in a central plateau that had somehow remained undamaged from the artillery bombardments, and then sat waiting for reinforcements to come and take the rest of the hill. I have no idea where Looky had stashed that flag.

I perched on a log seat, looking out over the open ground towards our own lines, while Looky and Winters checked some of the bodies that were littering the ground.

"A gas attack?" I asked.

Looky shook his head. "There would still be a stink in the air."

Winters looked up from searching a body on the far side of the clearing.

"If there had, we would have been hit too."

He looked back down at the dead man lying huddled against the sandbag wall of the clearing, and frowned.

"This body is still warm."

"What?" It was Looky's turn to be confused. He

walked over to where Winters was holding the dead man's wrist.

"It would be, wouldn't it? He's only dead a few minutes."

Winters glanced up.

"No, I mean really warm."

"We should go and find out what everyone else is up to, I'm sure they should all be swarming this place by now," I said, pushing myself away from the wall and walking over to where Winters knelt.

Shouts from our own men and screams from the dying could still be heard from the field below, but it seemed that we were the only ones to have reached the top of the hill.

Looky leaned down over the dead man with a puzzled look on his face. I had only crossed the clearing halfway when the body twitched.

The leg was the first to go. It was like a spasm, except slower. A cracking noise resounded over the clearing, a sound like thick branches breaking.

"Oh Jesus!"

Winters stumbled back away from the body as the second ripple of movement spread through it, bones cracking one after the other as the whole body writhed slowly. Winters reached back for his rifle, which he had slung over his shoulder while he searched the bodies, but Looky was faster.

"What the hell?" I said, reaching for my own rifle a second after Looky took a step back and raised his rifle. He was fast, that old guy, and moved out of range just as the dead man's arm shot out, his hand clenching like it was trying to grab a hold of him.

My ears were still ringing from the sound of guns and artillery, so when Looky blew the dead man's head half away, I barely heard it, but I did see the splatter of blood, brains and bones dash across the floor and up the sandbag wall.

The body twitched one more time before slumping motionless to the floor again.

"Did you just see that?" Winters blurted. He was gasping for air.

"He can't have been dead," I said, crossing the rest of the clearing quickly to stand by his side.

"He was dead," said Winters.

"You did say he was still warm," said Looky, kicking the body.

"You calling me a fool?"

"Of course not, but you did say he was a lot warmer than he should be."

Winters was about to speak again when I saw more movement on the edge of my vision. I spun round, rifle raised, and my nerves on fire, to see another of the bodies moving. This one was a little further down the slope, leaning against the sandbag wall.

"There's another," I said, moving towards what I had thought was a dead man, with my rifle held out in front of me, ready to fire.

"Wait," called Looky.

"Just shoot him Reggie," said Winters.

"No, wait."

Looky sounded insistent, so I moved forward, but held my fire, as he took a position behind me.

"What the hell are you doing Looky?" demanded Winters. I could hear him moving along the other side of the wall, behind me.

"You both saw how that last one moved, didn't you?"

I nodded, but didn't turn to face him, just in case the new moving corpse did something I wasn't ready for.

"So?" asked Winters.

Looky stepped past me and moved into a crouched position a few feet from the body, which began writhing and twitching, the bones breaking with every move.

"That ain't normal," I said.

"Exactly," Looky confirmed, "and I want to know why the hell it ain't."

I heard the sound of Winters cocking his rifle.

"Hold up. Wait," said Looky, raising his hand to command a halt. "Just wait damn you. If he gets up and comes at us, blow the shit out of him."

So we waited, as the body twitched some more and bones cracked. Then it lay there, still.

"Damn, that's strange," said Winters.

Then the body began to move again, using its broken arms to raise itself off the floor. Gradually it stood upright, and then turned to face us.

Half of the dead man's face was bruised and broken and it looked as though it was held together only by the grazed skin that hung from his face. His eyes had turned clear, almost like a blind man's, except they seemed translucent, almost totally clear. There was something very unusual about the way those eyes looked. They almost glowed.

"Wait," said Looky, I guess he was preempting Winters, because the old guy cursed. We stood there, all three of us with our rifles aimed at the dead man, as he looked back at us. Then he spoke, his voice deep and harsh, almost a whisper.

"You should be gone from this place, dying ones, before it is too late for you."

"What the hell do you mean?" said Looky, his voice commanding and loud. "You should be dead. I saw you dead, yet you're standing. Why is that?"

"You cannot know, dying one, you must not know."

It took a step towards us. The man's gun lay on the floor barely a yard from him, but he didn't seem at all interested.

"You come a step closer, and I'm gonna send you the hell back from where you came."

"Futile, dying one."

"Who the damn are you calling dying one? What

the hell are you anyway?"

Winters and Looky started backwards, keeping the distance between us and the dead man, I kept in line with them, but heard a noise behind us, that bone-cracking sound. I glanced across the clearing, and saw that at least a dozen other bodies, all the ones that were lying there, were contorting in the same manner.

"Erm.. I think we have a problem…"

"Not now Reggie," said Winters.

"No really, guys, you need to see this, there are more."

"You should leave before my master arrives," spoke that same deep, coarse voice.

A shot rang out, and as I was watching the man take another step towards us, half of his face just vanished. The body shuddered, unbalanced by the blow, then staggered backwards for a step before collapsing into the mud.

Across the clearing three of the other bodies were now pushing themselves to their feet. I glanced at my friends. Looky was reloading his rifle, while Winters backed away towards the slope where we had first cleared the summit of the hill.

"Should we shoot them?" I asked, unable to hide the fear in my voice.

"No point." it was Winters. "Look down there."

Behind him, down the slope that led into the warren of trenches, it seemed that the whole ground was alive with movement. The dead were rising, and there were many of them.

"Unless you've got a whole heap of spare shrapnel, we better just get us the hell out of here," Winters continued. "I know that I don't."

The three of us backed up to the far wall, against the sand bags that protected the clearing from the slope leading down into the field. Around us, nearly every dead man was slowly getting to his feet, excluding the two we had already dispatched.

Looky raised his rifle and took down the nearest two cadavers, while I aimed at another that was rising just ten feet away from us. Looky looked as nervous as I felt.

"Well boss, I hope you've got some bright plan, because apart from diving over this wall down a forty-foot drop to those rocks, I'm clean out," he said, shaking his head.

Just as Winters glanced behind him, looking out over the drop down into the field below, a doorway in a wall barely twenty feet away burst open, expelling two soldiers whose faces were pale, eyes wide with shock. They stumbled out into the light from the cavernous bolt-hole, and into the clearing, spotting us before I even had a chance to register that they weren't just more walking dead.

Looky only had time to curse and raise his rifle towards them before the first one opened fire on us, loosing off three shots before I could react. As I spun around, and fired on the shooter, I heard a grunt and

Looky disappeared from my peripheral vision. I feared the worst. My shot took the shooter full in the chest, and he staggered backwards, nearly knocking his companion over in the process, before falling over down the steps to the doorway they had come through.

As I struggled to reload my weapon, and the second soldier turned to face me, a shot rang out behind me, then another, and the remaining man crumpled to the ground, twitching.

Magazine refreshed, I ran forward, and put a final bullet into the first soldier, before running back to see how badly hurt Looky was. By now there were maybe two dozen of the walking dead slowly edging their way into the clearing, and I could see at least as many shambling up the slope from the trenches below.

Looky was dying. Hit directly in the neck by one of the shots. The second had gone astray, with the third taking Winters in the back of the leg. Looky's face was already turning pale, and he was struggling to breathe when I reached him. Blood pumped in hot torrents from behind his hands as he clutched at his throat, gasping for every breath that he could force down his throat.

Winters staggered over to us, and fell in a heap next to his old friend. Those two men had been through so much together. His face was stricken.

"No, no, no, you old tramp, don't you die on me."

"To late...boss, He...got me...a good one."

Every word was forced, his voice weak.

"Damn you John. This ain't the place. We were supposed to finish this together. You remember? Tea on the regent's, and sandwiches on Blackpool beach."

"I think...I might have to...pass...on the tea, boss. And I never...liked...Blackpool anyway."

"Don't you worry, John. I'll drink tea for both of us."

"You do that...for me, boss."

Moments later John "Looky" Wilmot ran out of blood. His voice grew raspier, his breathing slow, and his face strained. I watched two scenes unfold, one eye on my friends, and the other on the dead men walking, who were slowly approaching us now. Winters held Looky, cradling his friend's head as the old soldier took his last breath. His eyes glazed over and his shoulders sagged.

"We have to get out of here," I stressed, leaving it as long as I could before making the point. The walking dead men were now starting to cross the clearing towards us, closing in, and on their faces was a tortured look of murderous, pure hatred.

Winters nodded.

"Into the bolt-hole."

Winters hoisted Looky up onto his shoulder, and even with the wounded leg, carried him towards the hide hole that the now dead soldiers had unveiled to us. I would have helped him if I could, but someone had to watch out for us, and carrying three rifles wasn't easy.

Once in the hole I rammed the door shut, using several broken poles that had split away from a section of the wall that was collapsed. Two spades and half of a chair helped to bar the entrance. There was no other exit. It was just a small room, barely bigger than a good sized shed, with three bunks and a small overturned crate in the middle, probably once used as a table. There was a gasoline lamp on the table, still lit, and playing cards strewn all over the floor. The room looked like a makeshift home for maybe three soldiers, two of whom I suspected we had just killed. Where the last was, I could only speculate. I hoped he was one of the ones walking around outside.

I positioned myself opposite the entrance, sitting on the turned-over crate, while Winters hauled Looky onto the bottom of the bunks, before slumping down against them.

And we waited.

The first thud on the door came maybe a minute later, but it seemed like a lifetime. The door jarred only slightly, the spades and shafts of broken pole taking most of the blow. I got the distinct impression that whatever was hitting the other side of that door was neither alive nor very strong. With each thud came that familiar cracking sound as the cadaver's bones collapsed inside its dead shell.

It puzzles me why the bones of these newly

departed, but walking, corpses, were so brittle. They did move in a very strange fashion, so maybe that was the reason. That was my guess at least, that every move they took, every step forced upon the dead bodies by whatever strange and godforsaken thing that now inhabited them, was against the natural movement of a man. I think they shuffled in whatever manner they would have done in their previous bodies. It seems the only rational excuse I can think of.

Soon the single pounding of a fist or foot became many, until the door was nearly shaking on its roughly made hinges. I prepared for the worst, for the moment where my three magazines of bullets, whatever Winters had left, and the remaining rounds that our trigger-happy friend Looky had left, would be the only thing prolonging the time I spent on this earth. I settled myself, even at that young age, to be ready to face the almighty and try to account for my sins. That thought scared me.

But it never came.

A few minutes later, just as the last of the gas ran out in the lantern, and darkness came upon us, the pounding stopped. The door still barely held firm.

I waited for a few minutes before creeping to the door, to take a look through one of the cracks that had formed during the assault. In my thoughts I could hear Looky telling me to wait up, give it more time. But I was always impatient, and was soon looking through one of the thin hairline cracks, out into the light of the day. One more pound on that door and I would have taken it full in the face, and Looky was no longer alive to tell me to do otherwise.

Outside I could see them all, walking away back down the slope, towards the maze of trenches that wound all the way to the bottom of the hill, where only a few collapsed walls breached the twenty-foot jagged drop that separated the hill from the muddy flatlands pocked with shell craters.

As I watched, they slowly disappeared one by one into the shadows and the mist that gathered down the slope, until there was but one figure left.

He was a tall man. I hadn't noticed him before, standing motionless and looking up the hill as the dead men walked past him. I was about to go back into the shadows, give them more time to disperse, and hope that soon my fellow soldiers would come storming up the hill, to liberate what we had already liberated, when he walked up the muddy path about halfway, so I could just see his face, glaring almost into my soul, and directly into my eyes, and spoke.

"All will be accounted for," he bellowed, his voice raspy and thick, choking to force the sound out of vocal cords that I really don't believe were made for that tone.

So it came to it. The thing that has haunted me for so many years in my dreams. That face.

His one good eye was no more human than seeing the night sky staring back down at you, an endless hole of darkness that gave not a speck of light. It was almost as though someone had pushed them back into his head, like they were made of putty, the skin around the sockets dry and black. His skull was twisted somehow and elongated, and a scar that must have been an inch deep, ran straight down the other side of his face. I couldn't be sure, but I thought I saw small sharp pieces of bone jutting out from the crevice, like spines, or even teeth.

He stopped about halfway across the clearing and repeated those same words again - "All will be accounted for," though this time I wasn't sure if he said the words out loud, or I just heard them in my head. Either way, he didn't wait around. His face, for a moment, betrayed a look of what I thought might be fear. He had spotted something he didn't like, spun on his heals, and paced back down the path to disappear into the mist after the throng of dead men.

The second strange figure to come into view appeared before the door, dropping down from the mud verge that my hiding place was burrowed into. His boots made a dull thud as he landed in the mud, his legs bending sharply at the knees, bracing against the impact of the drop.

But this didn't slow him down. No, he paced across the clearing and followed the direction of the scar-faced man into the mist, and in moments he had also vanished.

Unbelievably, this man was more imposing than the gaunt, alien-looking first one. He was strongly built, his shoulders and arms bulked out from under his dark, worn garments. In his right hand he carried a weapon that I had not seen before, a rifle that looked similar to my own, but was constructed of a black metallic material - no wooden shaft or butt adorned this weapon. The magazine that stuck out from the bottom was bulky and long, maybe ten inches jutted out from the main body, curved forward in a strange arc.

Just before this second stranger disappeared from view into the mist, he took one sharp glance backwards, also looking straight at me. His features were pale, but not scarred, and he looked young, maybe only a few years older than me, but something in that alert glance told me that there were more years of experience in them than I would see in my entire lifetime.

He vanished from view, his long cloak flapping behind him for a moment before following him into the gloom. I sat there stunned, unsure of what I had just witnessed, confused, and scared as hell.

That day in the trenches was to be my last. As I staggered out of the bolt-hole about an hour later to greet the refreshing sight of allied troops heading up the slope, I found the third and last soldier who had lived in the hole. He had been in there with us all along, tucked under the bottom bunk, in a tiny space that a man could barely squeeze, quietly waiting for a time to leave safely. I can only presume that when he followed me out and saw the number of approaching enemy troops he gave up all hopes of escape, and resigned himself to death. But he wasn't going to go without a fight.

The bullet took me straight between the shoulder blades, and it was by luck alone that it missed every vital part of my body, barely chipping my spine. It exited out the front just below my collar bone, taking with it just a few small pieces of bone and muscle.

Moments before, I had been sitting, gazing down at almost that same spot, as I realised that not just Looky had died in that bolt-hole. The bullet that Winters had taken in the top of his leg must have hit an artery or something, because while I had sat there, guarding the door, he had slowly and quietly bled to death behind me, leaning against the bunk, his arm across the chest of his best friend. Although it saddened me to lose them both, I think it was fitting that they had died together, if they had to die at all. There wasn't a part of their world that hadn't involved the other one.

# 5

Now, do you remember how I was saying that most of the time folks would just pass you by, ignoring you, stuck in their own little world of problems, yet there were occasionally the odd one or two that were different?

Well, I met one of those folks in a field hospital about ten miles from the trenches, where I went to after that day on the hill. I was so glad to see that hill disappear from view, bu at the same time sad because of those I had left behind.

Between waking up in a field hospital, on a rough bed that I think was just there for me to die on, lying there in pain for a week before I was able to at least breathe without crying out in pain, and being shipped off back to England, conditionally discharged because of injury, I never saw those two old boys again. It's one of the things, and believe me there are many, that I truly regret in my life. Not knowing where they were laid to rest.

I made a remarkable recovery, the doctors told me. All they had done was clean the wound as well as they could and then stitch up the holes. I guess with that kind of injury, the most they could do was patch me up and hope. The doctors didn't promise me anything, saying that if I was strong, and rested, I might make it through. Of course, as I already mentioned, the wound was superficial. I didn't have to recover from much, except maybe the shock.

Soon I was bandaged up and hobbling around the sprawl of field tents, running minor errands for the staff. Nothing strenuous, that wasn't allowed, mostly it was just taking papers and messages backwards and forwards around the various parts of the camp. After a while, when I had gained the trust of many of the doctors in the hospital, they started asking me to take medical supplies.

It was simple. One of the doctors would tell me they needed such and such in one of the tents, which I would duly write down on a little notepad that I had acquired, and then waddle over to the stores shed, give them my list, and take them to wherever they were needed. Sometimes it was a cure, and sometimes it was, well, just something to ease the pain of passing.

That was how I met Joe Dean.

Born Joseph Henry Dean, 1885 in Brady, Texas, a place he claimed was the very heart of that county, and the soul of America. He told me how his fathers were the founders of the town. Well, I'm not sure I believed him, but Joe had a way of telling stories, there was something about his nature that just made you smile.

When I first saw him, he was looking sorry for himself, lying in one of the tents on the northern side of the camp, next to a man dying of tuberculosis. I was taking a bag of medical supplies over to the nurse who was attending that poor man. Don't ask me what they were, because I just did as I was asked.

Joe had the deepest Texan drawl you'd ever hear. I had met a lot of Americans in the camp, along with many folk of all nationalities, and I had difficulty telling one American accent from the other, but Joe's voice was so distinct that there was no mistaking where he came from.

I walked in, carrying my satchel full of bags and bottles, took one look around, and headed over to the nurse on the far side of the tent. I made it about halfway across before he spoke.

"Hey pal, you got any water in that schoolbag?"

As it happened I did, and he took it and drank down about a half before I could stop him, a whole lot of it spilling down his front and onto the bed, but he didn't seem to mind.

"You're a lifesaver. They don't look after us so good up here."

The nurse overheard him speaking and walked over to meet me.

"You giving this young man a hard time Joseph?" she said, with a look of mock disapproval on her face.

"I was just getting me some water, goddamn it, you see what I mean?"

The nurse was an older woman, maybe in her late forties, and still looking fine for her age. She glanced at me and frowned.

"Are you the man delivering my medicines?"

I nodded.

"Then come along, and don't you listen to that old soldier, he's all mouth."

I followed her over to a table on the far side of the tent, listening to Joe cursing all the way.

"Hey I'm a wounded man here, a bit of respect wouldn't go amiss now."

"Joseph Dean, you shut your chirping up now, there are men here that need more help than you do."

She looked at me, and shook her head as Joe continued to curse over in the corner, albeit a little quieter.

"Just ignore him. He's harmless enough, but he doesn't like it when he's not getting the attention."

After I had handed over my delivery I started to walk back out of the tent, past where Joe was lying, still complaining to himself about his treatment at the hands of his so called persecutors. Anyone else would have looked like a self-pitying fool, but his tone said something different.

"Hey schoolboy, you look a little young to be out here busting your ass, shouldn't you be in college or something?"

He was sitting up now, leaning against the back of the bunk, and smoking a cigarette that smelled like it was made of dried grass. Grey smoke wafted around and swirled in a plume towards the open entrance.

I stood for a moment, puzzled by his comment.

There were enough young men in the camp, and there had been a lot more of them in the trenches than I had expected, but no one had thought to comment on it.

"What's up boy? You slow or something?"

He smiled, a lopsided, cheeky grin that was infectious.

"No sir, I'm not slow, I just hadn't thought about being too young to be here."

Joe sat up, grimacing a little with the pain, and holding his leg, which, from the bandages wrapped around it, I presumed was the reason for him being in the tent.

"How old are you boy? You can't be above seventeen at the most."

I nodded. "Sixteen, sir. But my papers say I'm twenty one."

"How's that come to be? You change your papers so you could come out to this hell hole?"

"No sir," I said, shaking my head.

"No I didn't think so. That must make you a damn criminal."

"I was caught stealing sir, just some food and a newspaper though."

"Just? Stealing is stealing boy. I guess after this place you won't be doing that again anytime soon?"

"No sir."

He didn't look convinced, but that was okay with me. I started to head toward the exit but he called me back over.

"Hey, wait up, no need to be heading off so quickly now, is there?"

"I suppose not sir, but I do have my duties to attend to."

"You know folks around here don't you? I've been here a week and all I've had to read is a half torn comic book some dead guy left behind. If you could find me a newspaper or something it would be damn good of you."

I shrugged.

"I don't know if I can find one sir, I'm not supposed to take stuff. Stealing is stealing."

He smiled at that.

"Oh come on, there must be a few lying around in the officers' quarters, or one of those doctors must have one. It doesn't have to be the latest. Anything will do just to take my mind off this place and the moaning."

He indicated the bed next to him, where the dying man lay mumbling and coughing.

"He ain't the most interesting of company."

Joe reached back behind him and into his jacket pocket, taking out what looked like a half full packet of tobacco, and then waved it in my direction.

"I'll make it worth your while."

"I don't know, sir, I'll see what I can do."

"You do that son, and I'll have a few smokes here waiting for you when you come back. And maybe you might want this damn comic book while you're at it."

That sealed the deal. I knew exactly where there was a pile of newspapers. The surgeons in the south of the camp used old ones to soak up the blood from the floor of the operating tent, when they didn't have any hay or sawdust to throw down. I unloaded a stack of them from the back of the supply wagons at least once a week. It seemed that even though we were stuck in this hell and there weren't always enough medical supplies to go around, the folks back home still saw fit to be able to send the latest news spread.

Two days later, when the supply wagon came in, I asked the driver if it would be okay to borrow a copy. He was a friendly old guy, and was more than happy with an extra packet of field rations. Joe was as pleased as anything, and I walked away with half of a comic book, and a few smokes in my pocket. Quite a trade I'll say.

The next week I spotted a single copy of the *Washington Post* tucked in that pile, and earned myself not just a few smokes, but a bar of genuine American candy to go with it. I left the tent with a smile on my face, and I could still hear Joe's voice fifty yards away proclaiming his annoyance at whatever he had just read. Even so, the smile on his face when I showed him that paper was enough to make me smile right back at him.

The following weeks turned up copies of the *New York Times*, and more frequently *Stars and Stripes*, some military press thing that Joe found interesting. I never found him anything from his home state, but I think that just being able to read about what was going on back in America was enough for him.

I always found it strange, how we learn to adapt to our surroundings so easily. When you got used to the cries of the wounded and the dying, the field hospital wasn't so bad. My wound was healing up nicely, almost too quickly I thought, dreading the likelihood of going back to the front line when I was fit enough, and I had gotten to know a lot of the folks in the camp. Most of the doctors called me by my first name now, and even the surgeon general said hello to me if our paths crossed.

The doctor that I liked the best was an old, crooked-backed man called Major Elsmoor. He was in charge of the sicknesses on the camp: cholera, tuberculosis, foot-rot - we had pretty much every ailment you could imagine passing through the place on a daily basis. Unlike the modern hospitals of today, that field camp just couldn't provide a cure for a lot of things, so most of the sufferers would be drugged and left to die as peacefully as possible. I'm sure that if there had been a way to get them back to England they might have stood a chance, but the reality was that a lot of them would just die on the way.

Major Elsmoor was a strange man, but his constant chattering made me laugh. Quite often, when I delivered something to him, I would find him sitting in the corner of one of the tents chattering to himself. I know it sounds strange, but I warmed to the man. As soon as he saw me, he would snap out of his blathering and a smile would brighten up his face. He always seemed pleased to see me, and asked how I was.

It's odd that such a quirky and seemingly harmless old man could have been responsible for all those deaths.

My walking papers arrived not long before the end of the war. It seemed that some administration problem had happened back home, and someone, somewhere had discovered that a prison in London had been sending out young men far below the call-up age, just to free up space. Apparently they had been hunting down all of the underage conscripts for months, unfortunately discovering that most of them were now dead. I heard from the officer who spoke to me, though, that some had been sent back home, and that I was one of the last to be found. They had trouble finding me because I'd been away from the front and unofficially placed for the last few months as a helper in the field hospital. Apparently, so many of the men at the hill had died, and been unidentified, that most of the names of those men serving in that assault had been written off.

They'd lost me.

The officer seemed almost saddened to see me go. I don't know whether that was because they were short of hands in the place, or whether he was a little embarrassed to be giving a boy his ticket home, knowing that I should never have been there in the first place.

I was to leave on the next convoy out, along with a handful of patients who were fit enough to travel back to England, but not healthy enough that they could ever be sent back to the front line.

When I climbed into the back of the truck, my sack of meagre belongings over my shoulder, and three bars of chocolate and a packet of tobacco stuffed into my pockets that were a gift from some of the staff there, I was sad, sad to be leaving a place where I felt I was of use, only to be heading back to homelessness in that damn city. But I was also exuberant to be getting out of the war. It's the strangest thing, having mixed emotions.

I soon forgot all about that though, because as I pulled up the shutter on the back of the truck and sat down, I noticed a familiar face sitting opposite me.

"Well, well. Ain't that a thing," I heard in that deep Texan drawl. "Looks like I'm not the only one who got their walking papers." Joe Dean smiled from the seat opposite me.

I looked back at him, smiled, and glanced down at his left leg, still wrapped up tight, with a fresh bloodstain creeping through.

"Not so much walking from what I see."

"Yeah, boy, is that chocolate you got there?"

I laughed.

We talked about Major Elsmoor for a long time on that journey, which seemed to last for ever. We went back over the events that had led up to Joe's close scrape with death, and the unavoidable outcome. We both found it puzzling that a man like the Major, who was a doctor of amazing talent, could turn like that, even if he was quite an eccentric fellow.

It started two weeks before I left the camp to head back to England on the convoy. One day he was his normal chirpy self, jigging around the camp like he was in Sunday school, rather than a sprawl of dirty tents filled with the dying, then the next morning, when I went to his surgery tent, which was a small, barely standing square canopy that was open on two sides for most of the day, he was a little too quiet. I handed over the crate, which contained a new supply of some drug that he used a lot. I don't remember its name. I also took him a new set of surgical knives, which under most circumstances he would have been joyous about. That morning he just nodded at me, and continued reading from a small clutch of papers. They looked like they were a letter of some kind, but I didn't pry. Elsmoor liked his privacy. I'm not sure what was in the letter, but it can't have been anything good, because I'd never seen him so withdrawn first thing in the morning.

That was the day that the deaths started to happen.

From that day onwards, Elsmoor was the same, always quiet and withdrawn, like someone had just switched off a light somewhere and not bothered to turn it back on again. He spent most of his free time, which was very little in that place, sitting in his personal tent, behind his surgery, quiet as could be. Whenever I saw him sitting in his tent, he was still reading that same letter, over and over again, must have been a hundred times.

At first it wasn't really noticeable, but I did overhear a couple of the staff talking that evening, as I sat on the bank near the river eating my supper. One of the nurses, a woman called Sue, was speaking in hushed tones to a supply driver who was due to leave in the morning. I didn't hear the start of the conversation, but when I heard his name mentioned, my ears perked up like a rabbit hiding in a field. I must have been ten feet away, so I wouldn't have been the only one to overhear it.

"I think Doctor Elsmoor is not well," she whispered. "He just didn't seem himself today."

"What do you mean?" asked the driver. I think he was from the same part of the country as old Looky, except his accent wasn't as deep.

"Well he just seemed quiet today," she said, "and I don't think he is paying attention as he normally would. He administered a restful peace to two gentlemen today, and I'm not sure they were lost causes."

"Are you serious?" The driver's voice was strained. "That's wrong isn't it?"

"Well I don't know, you know how short of

supplies we are here."

"Yes, I deliver them, but putting down a man who could be saved."

"Oh, I don't know, they were both in pretty bad shape, and he said we needed to preserve what supplies we had for those who were coming in that could more easily be saved. I didn't question him at the time, but I feel terrible about it now."

"You should tell someone." The driver's voice was grave.

"I can't do that," came the exasperated reply. "He's the best doctor in the field, I'm wrong to question his practice in the first place."

"If he is a danger to folks..."

"No, it's not like that, he's just distracted at the moment, I'm sure he'll be fine."

"Well I hope you know what you're doing Sue, I wouldn't want you to get in any trouble just to defend the doctor."

I think Sue must have regretted bringing the subject up, because she backed off and changed the subject as fast as an alley-cat smelling a dog.

My thoughts drifted away from their conversation after a while, before I eventually turned in to sleep. It had been a long day, with a new batch of the injured arriving at dawn that morning, mostly diseases. It was amazing how we seemed to get more diseased soldiers than injured ones. But then I remember that field below the hill, filled with the dying after our assault, and the moans of pain that slowly stopped as each one of them passed into his fate. If you were shot out here that was you pretty much finished.

I woke up a little late the next morning, and was lucky that Elsmoor had gone about his rounds early, otherwise I might have had myself a little telling-off for tardiness.

The first I heard of it was as I arrived at the foremost tent in the south of the camp, not far from my little nook at the back of the barracks tent, and the first port of call for me most days.

As I was about to enter the tent, three soldiers with military police helmets rushed past me, heading north and away from the river, up towards the surgery tents, where all the most urgent cases were kept, including the new arrivals. It was unusual to see them off in such a hurry, strange even to see them in the camp in the first place. They were usually posted out over the bridge, at the gate. But this morning they hurried off up the hill and disappeared into the warren of tents and out of sight.

The ruckus started when I came back out of the tent with my first list of required supplies. I could hear shouts echoing down into the valley, and then chaos broke out. First there was a lot of shouting, which rose into a crescendo, until the final ear-wrenching gunshots resounded. I nearly dropped my notepad in my hurry to run up the hill.

I wasn't the only one making an urgent line for

the arrivals marquee, where all the noise was coming from. Nurses, doctors, and a few soldiers rushed out of tents from all directions and scurried up the hill.

When I got there I couldn't get into the marquee for so many people rushing around and shouting at each other, though I did catch a glimpse from the edge of the entrance.

The nurses and doctors seemed to be rushing to revive a number of soldiers lying in the bunks of the tent. They were minor injury cases, as far as I knew, but they didn't seem very minor now. Most of them lay there cold as dead, which it turned out most of them were.

In the middle of the room at least two doctors and a couple of nurses struggled with what I thought was a patient, but as I watched, I saw that pair of brown ankle-length boots that he always wore, sticking out from underneath one of the doctors who was trying to bring Major Elsmoor back to life. It was hopeless though. A gunshot wound to the chest and another to the head was quite the guarantee that Elsmoor was never going to breathe again.

I didn't find out much more about the incident until Joe recounted everything he had witnessed, while we sat in the back of the truck, heading away from the camp. Everyone had been closed-lipped afterwards, and the standing officer who took over the camp the same day, a tall, skinny man by the name of Renwood, who I think was another major like Elsmoor, gave the order out that the incident was not to be discussed by anyone until after an investigation had been made.

Joe had a little extra to tell me...


"I was lying on my bunk reading that newspaper you got for me the day before. I had just got past the news and into the sports section, which I always looked forward to, when Elsmoor came into the tent.

He was quiet as anything, and I said good morning to him, but he didn't pay me any attention. Just went about his business. I was a little put out by that, but he had been acting a bit strange lately anyway, so I just kept my mouth shut, and left him alone to do his work.

I thought it was strange that he was there so early that morning, and that he was the one giving out the injections, instead of the nurse. He just went along the line, stuck each and every man in the row with his damn needle, moving through each of them with an almost clinical precision and speed.

Then he got to me, and you know he looked at me for a moment before I realised what he was doing, I don't know how I did - it must have been that cold look on his face. He held the needle up for a second, watched me, and then said, "You don't want to go, do you?'

He was looking down at my leg and then back up, staring me straight in the eyes. There was something vacant about that look.

I was numb, shocked. I almost didn't open my mouth, though when he frowned at me, I eventually did.

'No thank you doc. I'm fine here.'

Stupid I know, but what else could I say? He nodded and then left, skulking out the door with his head low, the needle in his pocket, and his bag, that brown, cracked leather one he always carries with him, tucked under his arm. Of course I gave him about a half a minute to get out, before I started bellowing at the top of my voice, just so he didn't come walking back in and stick me one to keep me quiet.

Then the rest you already know about. It's a shame they had to do him in the end, but apparently when the MP's went in and told him to move away, to stop, he ignored them, and was just about to stick yet another soldier, one who just had a broken leg, and was lying there asleep."

After he finished, Joe sat there in silence for a while. We both did. It's so hard to imagine how a previously sane man could just go off the boat like that.

Major Elsmoor died from massive blood loss and brain damage about five minutes after he was shot. With him, he took a hundred and thirty-seven men - nearly a quarter of all the patients in the field hospital. I wish I knew what possessed him to do that. What was in that letter that started him off on that road?

Maybe it was just best left alone.

# 6

I met Marie again in a hospital north of London.

She was cleaning the floors of the ward where I took Joe. I wasn't meant to be there of course. My ticket home, and my time in the military ended the moment I stepped out onto the docks, but I had grown fond of Joe Dean, and I kept a promise I made to him, to travel with him until he was settled into the place. Being an American in England at that time was certainly nothing unusual, they were all over the place, but he didn't know anybody, and really, when I think about it, I didn't want to lose touch with him. I didn't have any friends myself either.

I stayed in the village just down the road from the hospital, and a strike of fortune gave me a job in a workhouse and a bed in the local hostelry at the same time. So I settled there for a while, spending my days working, and my evenings either sitting playing cards with Joe, or drinking in the pub down the road. I didn't earn that much money, but it was the first time in my life that I was paid to do anything. It was enough to get by on.

One evening I was playing cards with Joe when she just came round the corner. We stared at each other for what seemed ages before she finally spoke.

"Reggie?"

"Marie?"

I can't even start to explain how happy I was to see her again. It had been a long time, but it was just like I had said goodbye to her on that street yesterday. She told me all about how she had gone back to her parents and started school again, and how she had volunteered to work in the hospital. We spent hours and hours recounting the years that had passed. I told her nearly everything, just missing out the parts about walking dead men and rampaging, mad doctors.

She was even prettier than I remembered.

A month or so later Joe was ready to leave the hospital, so I packed up and headed back into London with him. He was why I was in the village in the first place, and it was good to see him on his feet at last.

Marie and I promised to keep in touch, and we did. I would travel to the hospital to see her every couple of weeks, and we would sit and talk after she finished work. I even went to visit her at home with her folks in Gravesend. This time I wasn't wearing rags.

From the accounts of the staff at the hospital, Joe was lucky to still have some use of his leg. The infection had been so bad that they nearly decided to cut it off to stop it spreading, but about a week after being in the hospital his health had turned around, the medicine they had been giving him started to work, and then it was almost like it had never been there. He was soon up and started walking, regaining strength in his withered legs. He built himself up faster than I would have believed, and I wasn't at all surprised when he said he was going to discharge himself and head into the city. He had plans, did Joe. Plans to open up his own coffeehouse, a Caff he called it.

"Just like they are at home, except this one will be in London," he would say. "It'll make me rich, boy. You'll see," he chirped, nodding to himself, "coffee and cakes in the front of the shop, whiskey and cigars out in the back."

I believed him. He had a way of instilling you with a sense of confidence, both in him and in yourself.

At first I wasn't sure where he was going to get the money from, but somehow he managed it.

"There's a few people owe me some," he said as we stood outside an empty building on Casey Street. It wasn't a big place, and the area wasn't the nicest in the city, but it was going cheap, and Gallowshill wasn't a slum back then - at least not for a few years.

We cleared the place out, and spent days hauling junk down the road to the scrap yard in Choke alley, just off Casey Street. I worked in his Caff for a while, just as he wanted, serving whiskey and all manner of strange imported teas out in the back room of the shop. Most times that room would be filled with a thick fog of cigar smoke, both day and night, and that dry, sweet smell of malt whiskey. I got to know most of the locals. Tad Bennet, the local cobbler, and

'Benny' to most of his friends, Ryan Cole, another American soldier who had set himself up just across the street with a small grocery shop.

The Caff was the place to go in the evening, for locals and for visitors, Joe was making a fortune out of the place, but I think somewhere along the way he got greedy, started doing deals out in the back yard, all manner of deals. He converted the small outhouse into a card den, and he had folks in there playing for money, and exchanging money for other things. This, of course, led to the trouble that eventually found its way into the place one night in mid-March, the night that Ryan Cole died, and the night that the leather bag turned up on the doorstep.

I was serving out the back, and it was about nine in the evening when Ryan brought the bag in. It was raining outside and it must have been sat on the doorstep for quite a while, because the leather was drenched through. He dumped it on the counter, and I was about to ask him to take it off when he spoke.

"Is this Joe's bag Reggie? I found it on the step just out there."

He nodded his head towards the back door.

I looked down at it, dripping dirty rainwater all over my clean bar, and shook my head.

"No, I don't think so, he's just out the back, I'll ask."

Joe was taking a smoke in the back yard, leaning up against the wall of the card den. He didn't like to smoke in the back room. He said there were already enough people smoking in there, and he didn't have anybody in the den at the time.

"Joe? Ryan's found this bag outside on the street, thinks it might be yours."

As I poured Ryan his whiskey, Joe stubbed out his smoke, walked into the bar, and just stood there next to me, staring at it. His face went from a ruddy brown to pale as snow. I'd not seen Joe look that shook up before.

"Where the hell did that come from?" he asked, throwing Ryan an accusing glance. "This some kind of joke?"

Ryan looked offended, "No, I found it outside there and thought it might be yours. I can take it away if you want. I'm sure Tad will pay a good price for it, looks in good condition."

"The hell you will," said Joe, and snatching up the bag, he walked into the office room that was just behind the bar, and put the bag square on the table with a thud.

Ryan looked at me, puzzled, and shrugged, handed me some coins for the whiskey and went to sit down in the corner of the room. He usually perched at the bar, but after the way Joe reacted he seemed a little put out.

I went into the office.

"You all right?"

"No, well, sure, yeah, look at this Reg," he said,

opening the top of the bag.

The whole bag was stuffed full of money - coins of all kinds, old, darkened and worn, like it had all been sat in someone's coat pocket for a decade, in the back of a wardrobe. But it would have had to have been one hell of a pocket.

"My god, there must be thousands in there," I said, "I've never seen so much money before,"

"I have," said Joe. "Just once."

I frowned at him, waiting for him to explain.

"This is exactly the same bag my money arrived in when I collected what people owed me, to buy this place, though I also borrowed a little at the same time."

"You borrowed money? How much?"

"Not too much, well, quite a bit, but nothing too worrying, and I never asked for any more."

"So what's this for?"

"I don't know."

Later that evening, as more folks turned up for their late night drinks, someone new stepped into the Caff. He was a short stubby man, wide of girth and round in the face, with a beard that seemed to go on for ever. He didn't look very old, but his beard was far too long for a young man.

For a man of such cumbersome build he moved with a careful grace that seemed unnatural, almost gliding across the floor of the back room and up to the bar, hardly losing his stride. I had a tumbler in my hand and a vodka bottle in the other.

He squared up to me, his face expressionless.

"Joseph Dean."

That was it, no please, no thank you, no explanation as to why he wanted to speak to Joe, just his name. I immediately didn't like him.

"No sir, I'm not Joseph Dean," I said. He irritated me in a way I couldn't place.

He sighed, squinting at me, probably just as annoyed by my answer as I was by his arrogance.

"I am aware that you are not Joseph Dean, Mr. Weldon. Now, please make him aware that I am waiting for him."

How he knew my name, I wasn't sure, and I didn't like that at all. But he seemed utterly humourless, so I decided that maybe I shouldn't agitate him. I put the bottle and tumbler down and headed out into the back room, where I thought Joe would probably be sitting in his chair, smoking.

He was standing over by the open window, looking out into the alleyway, smoking his pipe with his other hand firmly on the top of the leather bag when I walked in.

"Joe, there's this strange guy here to see you. I don't like the look of him, but he knows your whole name, and he looks pretty serious."

Joe turned to me and nodded. He paused for a moment, looking down at the floor, his hand still on the bag.

"Tell him I'll be out in a moment."

I did that, and the gentleman waited silently at the bar, refusing to take a drink or even sit down. He just stood there, looking around the room.

Ryan stood up and went to join Tad over at the corner table, throwing me a curious glance as he did so. I frowned back, and shook my head at him. I didn't know what this guy wanted, but I was sure it wasn't good, and I had a suspicion it was something to do with that leather bag that Joe was holding on to so tightly.

A minute later and Joe came out, dumped the bag on the bar and looked at the man.

"There is your money, I never asked for it."

"No I am aware that you did not ask for it. The money in there is equal to how much you must place into the bag to repay your debt to us."

"I don't have the money."

Joe put a hand on the bar, his pipe nowhere in sight.

"The agreement was for longer than a few months."

"At our discretion," said the gentleman.

"At your discretion? I expected a little more time than a few months."

"My employer has decided that your debt to us must be paid back immediately."

"I said I don't have the money. I need more time."

"This guy giving you a hard time Joe?" asked Ryan, who without my noticing was halfway across the room heading towards our guest.

"No Ryan. Leave it be, it all right."

"I'm quite serious Mr Dean. Your debt must be paid this minute."

"Hey didn't you hear the man? He said that he doesn't have the…"

What happened next was so fast, I'm not sure I even saw who shot who until my brain caught up with me. Our visitor spun round, his hand raised, a gun held firmly in it. Then Ryan flew halfway across the room, most of his head vanishing in that instant, splattering the windows, furniture and the back wall with blood. I'd barely managed to move out of the way, let alone think about doing something about it, when Joe's hand came up from behind the bar, revealing a shotgun that was already cocked. Our visitor had just enough time to turn back round to face us and give Joe a resigned look, when most of the upper half of his body disintegrated in the shotgun blast.

When the dust and noise settled I poked my head up from the bar, where I had ducked when Joe's shotgun went off, looked around and saw the destruction of the room.

Tad crouched over the body of Ryan, and then stood up. "Jesus!" he bellowed, from the corner. He had ducked down on the floor when the shooting had started, and from the chunks missing from the top of the table he had hidden under, and the splinters of wood that had showered that corner of the room, he had barely escaped injury himself.

"What the hell is going on?"

I saw him looking down at the floor, and my vision skipped over to Ryan, who was on the floor barely three feet from him, the visitor's body sprawled across the floor halfway across the room.

"He's dead," Tad looked pale. "They're both dead."

"You calm down now Tad," said Joe, turning to face me. "You going to help me clean up this mess?"

I nodded. And that's what we did.

Joe closed the place up, pulled all the curtains shut, and the three of us set to making our story as best we could, deciding that Ryan and our visitor had killed each other.

Soon the police were crawling all over the place, but our story seemed to be fine with them, and there were no conflicting stories to say anything different, I think that anyone that had heard the shots probably just ignored them, and most folks prefer to pretend stuff just doesn't happen. To be honest, I don't think they gave a damn. They seemed glad to know that the incident was over and that apart from getting the bodies removed and the whole cleared up, they didn't have a reason to stay.

They had James Alderman, the local undertaker, come over, and between us we cleaned up the place and boxed the bodies, which were then taken off in a police van to god knows where. James didn't say anything, but I could tell from his expression that he wasn't entirely convinced of our story. He never questioned it though, and he never said a word to anyone, not that I know of anyway.

By the time it was all cleaned up, and it was just me and Joe in the bar, it was nearly morning. I picked up our dead visitor's other weapon, a shotgun, which Joe had hidden out in the storeroom while the police had been there, and went to place it under the bar in the card den. I don't know why I noticed it. Maybe it was some strange instinct that made me examine it.

There, marked clearly on the barrel of the small cut-off shotgun, was a symbol I recognised. It was a small silver circle with the block letters HOLCROFT.

The police came back a few times after that, different ones, always asking the same questions over and over, and always seeming glad to leave. Things like this happened all over London in those days, at least in places like Gallowshill they did. I wouldn't imagine any of those police officers liked visiting the place very much.

They didn't find the shotgun. We hid it away in the beams above the card den, just where we would hide nearly everything that Joe dealt in that place. The gap in the ceiling was so well hidden that most folks didn't even suspect it was there.

After the police had made all the investigations they could, and grilled me with questions for the tenth time, they gave up trying to find out what really happened. No one was saying anything. I think the chief investigator of the case, a big man called Leyton, or something like that, had a clue that there was more to the story than was being told to him, but he soon got bored. There were enough murders in that part of London for him not to care too much about yet another bar killing.

For some reason Joe decided that I should keep the shotgun, if I wanted it. So I did, and I put it under my bed upstairs in the small back room that I had made my home, just above the pantry and next to Joe's room. I gave it a good clean-up, took off the Holcroft mark and threw it away. One last link to my past life removed and one more that I didn't have to remember.

We thought that was the last we were going to hear about it. The dead man was the one that Joe had dealt with to borrow the money in the first place, and it turned out he was the proprietor of a hard-arm lending company in Soho, one that the police had been itching to shut down for years.

Of course things don't always turn out how you hope. No one had considered that the lender had a partner.

About two weeks later, while Joe was out dealing with some business, and I was minding an empty bar, waiting for a delivery, a young boy, no older than I had been the day I floated away down the Thames and away from the auction warehouse, walked in the back door, looking a little frightened but hopeful at the same time.

He was shorter than I had been at that age, and a little fatter. I guess he knew where to get his work from, or he had a good master. It turned out that 'good' wasn't the appropriate word.

He edged forward, looking at me sheepishly, as I cleaned glasses with a bar cloth.

"Scuse me sir."

"Yes boy?"

"Are you Mr Weldon sir?"

"Who is asking?"

"Um, Mr Dean said I could find you here."

"Mr Dean?"

"Mr Joseph Dean sir, he said that I could find you here."

"Ok you've found me, now what does Joe need with a messenger?"

"Um, he said that if I asked you to take the leather bag to the old swimming pool, he would pay me a shilling."

"Really? A whole shilling, just to pass a message on to me."

"Yes sir."

"Now, that seems a strange thing to ask, don't you think?"

"Um, yes sir. But he said that the gentlemen with him would kill him if you didn't take it."

My heart sank at that moment, and I'm sure that to that young kid my face must have drained of all colour, because I could see his expression change from tentative to ready to run. I don't suppose he wanted to be delivering the message any more than I wanted to take that bag to the swimming pool.

"Who was with him boy?" I asked.

He scratched his head and frowned.

"Four men, I think, sir. One of them was really, really big as well. They all had guns, all but the big man I think."

"Right. And they have Joe in the swimming pool?"

"Yes, he is all tied up and lying on the floor in the bottom of the pool. I think they beat him up, sir."

"Right, well here is your pay."

I gave him two shillings, to which his eyes widened.

"The second is so that you don't say a word to anyone."

"Yes sir," he said, itching to leave.

"Not a word to anyone, you hear me?" I called out as he ran out of the door.

It took me half an hour to get over to the swimming pool. It could have taken me half of that, but part of me didn't want to go, even though the other part knew I wasn't going to leave my friend to be killed.

The leather bag was still where Joe had stashed it,

still full, and tucked into the back of the wooden cabinet in the office, stuck behind a pile of books. The cabinet was another of Joe's little hiding places. It was built with a hidden compartment that was so well made you never would have suspected it was there, and if you did there was only one way to open it, with one key. Both of the drawers had to be open at the top, yet both locks had to be firmly locked. Only then could you pull the panel out.

When I lifted the bag I knew something was different straight away. It was heavier, much heavier. I took a moment to open it, and by my estimation there must have been twice as much money inside the bag as when Joe first showed me. From somewhere, Joe had found the money to match what was in there, just as the dead lender had demanded.

I stood for a few moments, outside the main doors to the old swimming pool, got my breath, swore that I should have taken my shotgun with me, and then pushed my way in, past the entrance.

There was a foyer just inside the main doors. Old white tiles, now smashed and greyed through years of dust and neglect, were scattered across the ground. Rubbish had collected in the corners and up against the railings, from where people had used the place as a dumping ground or a squat over the years. Where there were once three rows of nicely polished wooden benches, there was now just a pile of broken wood and glass. The huge panelled glass that allowed you to see into the swimming baths from the foyer were long gone. Just a few fragments stuck out from the rotten wooden frames like sharpened teeth.

Through the gaping hole that had once been the panelling I could make out the faint light of several oil lanterns. They were the only visible light. Once nearly the entire roof had been clean glass, to let the sunshine in, but at some point, when they had all been broken, someone had boarded all the holes up, cutting off the light from the outside world. The baths had fallen into darkness, and the damp warm wet had encouraged mould and rats to spread through the building.

I couldn't see Joe, but I could see two men pointing rifles down into the sunken depths of the swimming pool. Another gentleman was sitting on the broken frame of a wooden crate, watching me. The fourth, the bigger man that the boy had mentioned, was nowhere to be seen.

"Come in Mr Weldon," chirped the seated man, his voice high, almost shrill. Like the others he was wearing a suit, except his looked more expensive, and he wasn't wearing a long trench coat like the two riflemen.

"May I ask to whom I am speaking?" I asked, waiting in the gap between the broken window frames.

"You may. I am Mr Blake, and I was John Whelan's associate, before his...demise." I noticed his eyes were on the bag.

"I see you have Mr Whelan's bag."

"I do."

"May I see it?"

He must have sensed my hesitation.

"Please Mr. Weldon, we mean you no harm, your involvement is…unfortunate, but necessary, do come in. "

I stepped through the broken frame and walked out over the tiles towards them. As I reached the edge of the pool, I saw Joe.

He was tied up, his hands and legs hitched together, as though he was an animal ready for slaughter. Standing next to him, with huge, meaty hands at his sides, was a giant of a  man. He must have stood over seven feet tall, even bigger than Chef from the Running Ground, but his height wasn't the biggest part of him. I think if you stood three men next to each other then you may have had the kind of bulk that was this man's body. He was dark skinned, and dressed in a perfectly clean and tailored suit. I think he could have wrestled an elephant, but there was something else about him that set me on edge, something wrong, something I couldn't place.

I passed the bag to Blake, who opened it for a moment, nodded to the two riflemen and made a short coughing noise, then stood up.

"That will do just fine, Mr. Weldon."

He turned and walked to the edge of the pool and look down at Joe.

"Mr Dean. Your account has now been satisfied.

We are pleased to have been of service too you. Do feel free to contact us at any point should you require our assistance once more."

And then they left. First Blake, followed by his two armed cronies, and then a minute later the big man down in the pool walked quietly away from Joe's crumpled form, climbed up the ladder at the side of the pool, and then passed me. He stepped through the broken panels, through which he had to stoop to get under, then out of the front doors.

I stood watching the huge man as he went out of the doors, all of the time trying to figure out what it was about him that was wrong about him. Then just as he stepped out into the light of the street and I caught my first clear look at him, just for a moment, I saw it.

His feet.

Where the other gentleman had worn new, shiny shoes, this man wore none. But then you probably couldn't have bought shoes for his feet. Because not only were they large, but they weren't even feet. At the end of his powerful legs were hooves.

Hooves, just like a bull would have, or a ram or something, or like the feet of something much darker, something that at the time I didn't even want to consider. At first I thought his feet had been cut off, and what I was looking at were the stumps, but in the thin shaft of light that shone on them from the doorway it was quite clear exactly what they were. I only saw them for the briefest of moments, and then he was gone.

They had beaten Joe up pretty bad. He could barely walk by the time I managed to untie and pull the ropes from him. He didn't say a word, just nodded at me and then stayed silent as I helped him back over to the Caff. I offered to take him to the hospital, but he shook his head. All I could do was take him up to his room on the top floor of the Caff, and help him into bed.

They hadn't broken any bones, or even cut him, but as I helped him take his clothes off and get into bed I saw that nearly every inch of his body had been beaten, and would soon turn bruised.

Joe didn't come out of his room for three days. I took food and water to him, making sure he was okay, but he lay there in the dark, with the curtains drawn, in silence.

When Joe finally came out a lot of the bruises had cleared up, but he looked pale, not his jovial self. He was still quiet, and withdrawn, and for a while he didn't say anything, just poured himself a large whiskey and sat just inside the doorway. When he did speak his voice was strained. Joe had a very distinct voice, and this didn't seem like the same man.

"I just wanted to say thanks for coming over there."

"That's fine, Joe. You would have done the same."

"No really, you could have left. You risked your

life, and I'm grateful."

I poured him another whiskey and placed it on the stool next to him.

"You're welcome Joe."

And that was the last we spoke about it.

Joe closed the place up for a few weeks, and during that time I found myself a new job over at the leather-cutting factory, as a clerk, counting receipts and making out orders and such. Joe knew the owner, and to be honest I think he was glad to get me out from under his feet and replace me with a young lady from south London who he had taken a liking to.

After a while I stopped going to The Caff as often and spent most of my time between my new job and visiting the hospital where Marie still worked.

Isn't it amazing how your life just changes all of a sudden, sometimes? I don't know what prompted it, but that would be the last I saw of Joe Dean. I guess sometimes our lives just move on. Mine certainly did. I was seeing a lot more of Marie during those days. Some changes are joyous, and often unexpected, but sometimes things don't work out exactly as you had planned, do they?

# 7

It was 1923, and we had been married for three months and two days when we set off on our trip to Edinburgh. It was a very different place back in those days. Even though a lot of people were struggling just to get by, living on the poverty line, post war industry was booming.

We left London at ten in the morning, almost on the dot, aboard the Special Scotch Express train out of King's Cross station. It was a bitterly cold morning and the fog was starting to creep in. I remember standing in that station, a chill in the air that penetrated to my bones, marvelling at what advances in engineering had come to pass to see such an impressive piece of machinery let loose upon the world.

I was still a very young man back then, and I had only been on a train twice before in my life, and both times it was to a place a lot less pleasant than Edinburgh, and in decidedly less pleasant company, so I was looking forward to that journey immensely.

It was one of the most extravagant things I ever paid for during my younger years, but of course, as I sat in that carriage with my new wife, watching the countryside go by at a leisurely pace, I wasn't to know at the time that I was to pay for that trip with more than money.

The train stopped at York for just a few minutes, to give the crew time to check the engine, and for the passengers to catch some fresh air. Then off we went again, thundering along the tracks towards our destination.

My wife and I sat looking out of the window for most of the journey. You have to remember that although a lot of it looks the same, most of the countryside that we were passing was completely new to us. I commented to Marie that we had watched the weather change at least half a dozen times in those few hundred miles. It seemed that the closer we got to Scotland, the brighter the weather was.

At six thirty in the evening we finally pulled into Waverley station, after a journey of no less than eight and a half hours. That might seem like a long time to you. Trains back then didn't travel at the lightning speeds they do today. But to a young man in the 1920s, the Special Scotch Express was a miracle of progress, and I was on an adventure never to be forgotten.

Stepping off that train, we were greeted by a whole new world - at least that's how we saw it. The differences between Edinburgh and London at the turn of the century were so many that only the sprawl of buildings made it the same. There was just as much squalor and dirt about the place, but the architecture was something completely different. I am by no means an expert at buildings, but I think you might agree that there is something in the architecture of a city that gives it its character, its personality. London always said to me 'I'm busy', whereas Edinburgh smiled and said 'welcome'.

The next day we took a carriage and toured around some of the more tourist-friendly parts of the city, and then lunched on Princes Street. We saw the Scott monument, and the Ross fountain, and then finally, before we retired to our hotel, Marie suggested that we take a walk along the canal. It was still quite early in the day, and the weather was very fine, so I agreed.

That walk along the canal was to be the last time I spent with my wife.

I noticed a change in the weather almost as soon as we stepped off the coach. There was a slight chill in the wind that hadn't been there all day, and for the first time in our visit I buttoned up my coat, and suggested Marie do the same. We agreed with the driver that he should meet us about half a mile along the canal. He said he knew a good spot to wait. We didn't know the area, but there was only a single pathway running along the edge of the water, so it seemed a simple enough arrangement.

The water was darker along this stretch of canal than I had seen elsewhere, and the trees cast shadows over the water that moved with the ripples. It was slightly cold, but we soon warmed up when we started walking.

I remember vividly that all along the edge of the canal was a mass of bright blue flowers, all no bigger than a few inches tall, and the flowers very small, but the area they covered spread out along the water's edge like a huge blue lawn. I also remember thinking how pretty they were, and how unusual it was to see them grow along the edge of the canal, and remain untouched. No one had seen fit to clear the area. I wondered what those flowers were called. Marie had a name for them, but I can't recall it now. It's strange how I have forgotten that.

We were about halfway along the walk when it happened, and I'm still not sure to this day if I can explain any better to a stranger than I could to the local police, and then after that the local magistrate.

It was quite simple really. We were talking about what our plans would be when we got back to London. I had decided I would take up an offer that had been made to me, to work as a training accountant for one of the big city lenders that a friend of mine was a worked for. I wasn't so keen on the idea, but I knew the work would be easy and it would pay well. Most men coming back from the war wouldn't be quite so lucky.

Marie was walking just behind me and to my left, just a little further away from the canal. The mass of blue flowers had spread out thicker along that small stretch of the bank, and she insisted we didn't step on any of them, so we walked single file for about fifty yards. Or we would have done.

She had started telling me how she thought that she would do well to go to work in the ladies' hair salon that was just around the corner from our home. At that moment we were about ten yards from the end of our single-file walk, and she disappeared, just like that. One moment she was there, and the next, she might have never existed.

I had seen her from the corner of my eye, and every few yards I glanced back just to check that she was okay. I was turning my head towards her, to do just that, when she simply vanished right before me.

There was nowhere for her to have fallen, nowhere for her to have quickly ducked behind to hide if she had wanted to play a little fun with me, and there wasn't even the slightest of sounds. All that was left behind was her scarf, the one I had bought for her from the market in London a few weeks ago. It had been wrapped tightly around her shoulders at the time, but now it drifted slowly to the ground to settle upon those blue flowers.

It took me a little while to comprehend what had happened. Well, maybe comprehend isn't the best of words, because I don't think I ever really understood what or why. I guess I mean that it took me a while to realise that she hadn't simply hidden somewhere. She was gone.

I ran the distance left between the spot and the driver, not thinking to pick up the scarf on the way, and came back with him scurrying along behind me. He was an overweight man, and it was quite clear from the way he was sweating and coughing his lungs up that running was not something he was used to.

The scarf was still there, and there was still no sign of my Marie. Even her footprints in the grass ended with her right foot forward and nothing in the other direction except the trail of her footprints that led back in time to the moments before, when she had been here, walking beside me.

We raised the alarm, called in the police to find out what was going on, and they arrived quite quickly…in droves. By six that evening I was in a cell at the police station, and by eight I had been officially accused of murdering my wife. They expected to find her when they dredged the canal. I tried to point out to them that she had only been gone a short while, but I got the impression they didn't believe a word I was saying.

As I sat there alone in that cold damp cell at the police station, waiting to hear something from the search, I was almost hoping they would find something. Had I just not heard the splash as she had fallen in the river? I don't believe that was it. She had been at least three yards from the edge of the water. But if she turned up dead in there, then I at least would know it was just a moment where I missed something.

They never did.

Not a single shred of evidence was to be found to say she had fallen in the canal and they searched nearly three miles of it. They tore up those beautiful blue flowers, and dug over the area, but there was nothing to be found of my Marie.

So they released me. One of the officers in charge of the investigation wanted to charge me with wasting police time, and suggested that Marie had never even been there, but the driver of the coach accounted for her, and there was very little else they could do. Except give me back the things they found at the spot where she had vanished.

The scarf was the first, then a gentleman's pocket watch, a small key ring with a pretty silver dolphin inscribed on it, a wedding band made of gold, a single brown leather glove, and a half-empty packet of cigarettes with a flint cigarette lighter stuffed into the packet as well.

Does that list sound strange to you? No, you might believe they were just some of the other things she might carry with her, except Marie never smoked, not once in her life, and she didn't much like the fact that I did either. She also didn't like leather, and she carried her keys in her purse, never on a key ring, and the wedding ring that I had bought for her was plate silver. We just couldn't afford something as extravagant as a gold ring.

And what about that watch? Well, the time had stopped at four fifteen, which could well have been about the time that she disappeared, except that the watch was rusted and damaged beyond repair. I know this because I took it into a repair shop, back on the Prince Street, and they told me the thing was at least forty years old. The company that made them went out of business twenty years ago. I wouldn't even be able to find the parts to fix it without paying a fortune to have them hand-made.

Do you see where I'm going with this? Well if not then let me spell it out to you. That place where Marie disappeared, I went back there two weeks later, and I went back there again for days after that, searching, always searching for that lost lady who should have been by my side.

Do you know how long it took me to find something? It took me two years. Two long years of hunting the streets of the city and walking the canals to find any sort of lead on what had happened. Oh I knew what those other things that were found insinuated, but I had to find something else. And then I did, right on the spot where she had disappeared in the first place.

It was a cold morning in December, and for some reason I decided to walk the same route that we had taken that day, all around the sights that we had visited that day. I even had lunch in the same cafe, and took a carriage out to the canal, telling the driver to meet me down the road. Everything just as it had been back then.

In the two years that had passed a lot of the area had grown over again. The police had stripped it all in their search, but it hadn't taken long for the same plants to push their way up from hiding, including those blue flowers.

I knew exactly the point where I had lost my Marie. I felt the same chill down my spine that I had felt the second that I had seen her disappear. I stepped over the spot where two years ago her footprints had ended, and into the space that she never reached. And I found something.

Lying amongst the flowers, almost out of sight, was a single hair pin. Just like the ones that my wife used to wear, only this one was a little more elegant and expensive than one that she could have owned.

Once more I noticed a set of footprints in the mud, ending at exactly the same spot that Marie's had. And I knew my worst thoughts were right. Someone else had gone to wherever it was that my wife had gone, just as those other people had, each one leaving something behind, maybe something given to them recently, that hadn't been theirs long enough to stay with them.

I know exactly what you are thinking, and don't you think I tried following her? I walked backwards and forwards on that spot for hours, and for the first few months I came back there day after day. And now my suspicions were confirmed. I did all that over again, just hoping that the door was still open, that I could step through, and follow those footprints, even though I had no idea where they might lead.

After two years I was at the very edge of my sanity, and in the end I broke on that canal bank. I had lost everything I owned in pursuit of Marie - the rent on the flat in London had run out, and the job that I had been offered was given to someone else. I had the rest of our money sent to Edinburgh, and as each day went by, the funds grew smaller and smaller.

When I eventually stood up and walked away from the canal bank for the final time, I walked away carrying everything I owned - Just the clothes I was wearing, my empty wallet, and a single return ticket to London that I hoped was still valid. There was a time for searching for Marie, and there was also a time to stop, but I didn't recognise it until I had lost everything in search of the impossible.

I caught the next train back to London, and I have never been back to Edinburgh since.

# 8

The second time I returned to Gallowshill was in the summer of 1926. Joe's Caff had shut down months before, and I hadn't seen anything of him for a long time.

Over the years following the war, Gallowshill had turned from a thriving new community into a den of thieves, homeless people and thugs. Everybody who had nothing seemed to end up there, taking from others around them who had just as little. Poor soldiers came back from the war, and with nowhere to go, they looked for places to work, and often found themselves in Gallowshill. It deteriorated over just a few years and had gradually become one of the last places you should be at such a late hour.

I didn't intend to be walking through for more than a couple of minutes. But that was enough.

I was just coming off the bridge and walking into Gallowshill on my way to the baker's house along the Thames when it happened. I wasn't paying attention, and by no means should I have been walking down that alleyway at that time of the night by myself. Maybe in central London I was safer, but not there. I guess I still hadn't learned that many lessons, and was still a little naive.

I felt a sharp pain in the back of my head for just

a moment, and then everything went dark. I awoke what I believe was a couple of hours later, with my boots, coat and hat missing and my wallet, even though it was empty, taken too. I had bled quite a lot, and was lucky to even still be breathing.

Struggling to stand, my head thumping from the pain, I staggered round the corner, along Casey Street, to the only place nearby that I thought I might be able to sit in peace for a moment: Joe's Caff.

It was closed, but the key to the back door was where it had always been left, in the guttering just above the back window.

The lock was stiff, probably rusted, but with a bit of effort I forced it open and staggered into the darkness of the old smoking room.

Where once the room had been plush and tidy, filled with oak tables and old leather chairs that Joe had bought cheap from a pub that was closing down a few streets away, there was now just a pile of rubbish and broken bottles. The door into the front shop had fallen off its hinges at some point, and now lay in the middle of the room, a wide split down its centre.

The place was a mess, and I stood there for a few moments, shaking my head, unable to believe that all of the work we did all those years ago, tidying up, cleaning, laying tiles and decorating, had all come to this, to nothing but ruin.

Pulling the door shut behind me, I hunkered down on one of the few remaining chairs. It sat legless on a pile of mouldy carpet just to the right of the entrance, the leather torn and frayed, cotton stuffing spilling out onto the floor.

When I came back from the war with Joe, I had high hopes for a life that would change, and for a few years they had. Joe had his coffeehouse, his Caff, and I had my Marie. All of that had gone now. Here I was sitting in the ruin of both of our dreams, with no boots, no wallet, nothing, and everything that I had of importance in my life was now gone.

I stayed in the Caff for a couple of days, quietly trying to get my head together, trying to decide what I was going to do. Gazing out at the street, or up at the noose which hung from where once there had been a chandelier.

I don't know who had put it there. I can guess that maybe in some moment of his life Joe had decided that he'd had enough, and hung it up there, ready to say his goodbyes.

He hadn't hanged himself, though. I could see that. The noose was untouched, still a fresh knot where the rope was wound around itself just above the hoop itself. The rope wasn't compacted like it would have been if it had been used. So what he had decided in the end I didn't know, but whatever it was, it took him out of that place and along another road.

I contemplated the very same things as I sat there that evening, and I think, I hope, that I made the same decision that Joe had - to start again. I wasn't finished fighting this world yet.

It started off as just a way of making enough money to buy food every day, clearing up other people's rubbish. I slept in the same bedroom above the Caff every night and pretty much made the place my home. What with Joe no longer around and the Caff closed, I didn't see the harm in turning the place into my little workshop, my storage room and shop front for selling junk. It all began with odds and ends, mostly scrap collected from the alleyways that I normally would have taken to the junk yard down Choke alley. But the very first time I hauled a cartload of metal down there to trade for a few coins, I found it closed.

Tad from over the road came over occasionally, and he said that the police had caught the old owners dealing guns out of the back yard, and busted the lot of them. He hadn't seen Joe since the night he closed the Caff up.

Over the next few years, Gallowshill started to change, yet again. Where there were empty tenement buildings with boarded-up windows, folks were rebuilding and tidying up the neighbourhood. All kinds of new businesses started to fill the old ruined storefronts along the main stretch, even right up to the Caff. As folks moved in I came along and offered my services. With the help of a few young men who were all ex soldiers like myself, I would completely strip out and clear up an old building. Furniture, junk, broken glass, everything, and of course while we did that, we picked up a hoard of other junk. Quite often they were things that folks might buy if they were cleaned up.

The Caff, which I renamed The Old Caff Trade Shop, was filled from wall to wall with it. Bicycles and bicycle parts, disused sinks, chairs, sofas, books, even window frames and doors. Anything that could be cleaned up and put up for sale, was.

By the time I hit thirty years old, I was wealthy enough to invest my money into buying my own place.

So the Old Caff Trade Shop became The Old Caff Trade Company, and it had a massive store frontage with tenement flats above it, just around the corner from Merriwether Avenue, not far from Piccadilly. I also bought the huge plot of land just at the back of the building. It was quite a substantial plot that was run down and disused. I think the local councillor was glad to be rid of the land, since he said that vagrants used it as a hangout, and I didn't really mind them, in fact, most of them cleaned up pretty good and worked very hard in the scrap yard that I put there.

Everything that I couldn't renovate and sell in the shop went out on that land, where the ex-vagrants ran it for me like any other scrap yard. You know, one time we even had a bus sitting on that land.

Yep. A genuine London bus.

A guy named Meril found it. It was abandoned about two miles away, which was dangerously close to The Running Ground for me, but whoever put it there had left the keys in the ignition, so I just jumped on in that seat and drove it across London, right into the yard, and tucked it away in behind a huge pile of bicycle and vehicle scrap.

At one point I was going to put a building up in the middle of that yard, you know, build myself a house there and clean up the area around it. I even got the yard boys to put up some scaffolding, right where I was planning to build. Well, you know things are. That house just never got built. I think I changed my mind and decided that I didn't want to live in the middle of a scrap yard. It makes me laugh really. I don't know how long that scaffolding stood there, because it was still there when I eventually sold up. Could still be there for all I know.

Even though my business was thriving, I still missed The Caff. It had been strange leaving it behind. I remember standing outside for about an hour after boarding up the windows, just standing in the dirt and dust of the road looking up at them. The place looked so forlorn when you covered up the windows.

As I stood there, all the memories of the place flooded through my mind, the times I spent serving drinks to familiar faces, playing cards out in the den at the back, and all the work me and Joe put into cleaning the place up at the beginning. I stood wondering to myself where Joe had wandered off to, and whether one day he would come walking back along the street.

Also I wondered what would become of the place now. There was no one to live in it, no one to keep the place from falling apart, and no one owned it apart from Joe. The Caff would probably sit empty for years, at least until someone discovered that there was no owner.

As I walked back along Casey Street, I passed the swimming pool. The alleyway along the side of the vast building, called Tinkers alley by the local folks, was, as ever, littered with refuse that was spilling over from the bins. Perched intermittently against the walls were the cardboard huts that had always been there, an ever-changing and shifting village of makeshift dens that the homeless of Gallowshill called home. About halfway down the track a group of ashen faced men stood over a metal bin, sparks of flame creeping out of the holes and licking up the inside as they fed the fire with bits of rubbish and wood. They were drinking from dirty bottles, probably some nasty homemade brew or industrial cleaner, and leaning on each other, blabbering their usual mindless drivel and arguing with no one in particular.

I had seen this scene dozens of times, and although the occupants of the alleyway changed over the years as new people drifted around and older residents died, the place always had the same desperate squalor. How close had I come to becoming one of those poor fools? How near had I already been a few times in my life to drowning myself in self-pity and foul-smelling liquids, just to dull the senses and ease the pain?

As I stood there in the middle of the road, gawking at the ugly scene before me, I noticed something else, something out of place, and it was only because one of the tramps hobbled over and stumbled to sit down on the broken wall that ran along the back of the swimming pool building, near the maintenance entrance, that I noticed a previously invisible part of the picture, that I noticed him.

At first I thought it was merely a pile of cloth, maybe a sack of rubbish that had gone unnoticed by the denizens of the alleyway.

Then I saw the blood.

Lying in the dirt, barely ten yards behind the burning barrel, where the tramps still continued their raucous laughing and drinking, was a body, and there was something strange about it that I couldn't yet place, something familiar enough that I couldn't just walk away, believing it to be just the latest death in the alleyway. The feeling was enough to make me change my direction and walk, for the first time, down into the nastiest and most dangerous lane in Gallowshill.

I made my way slowly along the track, weaving between the ghetto of cardboard cells, stepping over broken bottles and human waste, avoiding the rotten carcass of a dog that was long dead and almost unrecognisable. I skirted around the drunken tramps, who barely even registered my existence, and made my way over to the body.

From ten feet away I could see that whoever this person was, they were still alive, and still breathing. As I got closer I could see the rise and fall of the person's chest as it heaved, a hoarse, gargling noise erupting with every desperate gasp.

It wasn't until I knelt by the injured man that I recognised who it was. The huge frame, the ragged black cloak, the young looking face covered in dried blood.

Well over a decade had passed since I last saw this man striding off into the mist of the trenches, following the horde of dead men and their gaunt ghoul-like leader to god knows where, as I watched, terrified, from my hiding place in the bolt-hole.

I had known even back then that this man's task and his duties had to be of great importance for him to follow such a monstrous army alone. Where had they all gone? Where was he? Who was the demonic thing that took all those men from the battlefield? Who was he? Where had he come from?

On this warm morning as I walked away from Casey Street for what I believed would be the last time, as I turned my back with the hope that by leaving it behind, I would also be letting go of the pain of my past life, a ghost from the past stepped back into the light.

I wonder sometimes if I should have turned away, left him to die, allowed the questions to go unanswered, but I always came to the same decision.

Fate.

Fate had put me there that morning. It had carved my path, from the trip to the bakery that I had never finished, to the strike on the head and the robbery that threw me into Gallowshill's dark streets once more. It had all happened for a reason, every step of it leading me one step closer to standing next to this strange man who needed help.

He was barely conscious as I helped him to his feet, hauling his arm over my shoulder. I was amazed at his size. I think if I had been ten years older I wouldn't have even been able to hold his weight. He was at least a foot taller than me.

We staggered, the two of us, him almost unable to control his own feet, and me struggling to bear his weight on my shoulders, back out of the alleyway and onto Casey Street. One of the tramps who was leaning against the broken wall, finished heaving his guts up and turned in time to see us pass. He struggled over to us and made a fumbling attempt to reach into the stranger's pockets. I couldn't stop him, so great was the stranger's weight. I would have had to drop him to the ground. But as he began to lower his arm, he glanced upwards at the tramp, who slurred some drunken words while still trying to slip his hand into one of the deep pockets of the stranger's coat. A moment later and the stranger's free arm shot up towards the tramp's face with startling speed, his bloody, broken hand clenching into a fist at the last moment, just before the impact smashed the tramp's face apart.

I heard a sickening crunch of bones and watched, stunned, as blood, teeth and bits of bone sprayed out behind the man. The punch lifted the drunk an easy five feet off the ground. He disappeared behind the broken wall and crashed back down on top of a pile of rubble.

I didn't stop to find out if he was still alive. Instead I continued hauling the stranger out of the alleyway, his moment of violent clarity gone, and his consciousness drifting once more.

"I need to get you to a hospital," I said, but as I turned left to head towards the nearest hospital, he spoke.

"No, please, no doctors."

His voice was strange, and I couldn't place the accent. It was English but tinged with something that I had never heard before, a deep undertone that was no accent I recognised.

"You'll die if someone doesn't fix you."

His chest heaved with the strain of talking, and fresh blood trickled out of his mouth, dribbling down his cheek as he coughed violently.

"No, I just need rest, please, hide me."

"You'll die if I don't take you to the hospital."

"No, please, no doctors."

I found this odd, and my instinct told me to ignore him, to take him to Drake Lane Hospital, just a few streets away, near the river. But I didn't. Instead I hauled him back down the street and into the only place I knew that I could hide him without fear of discovery. The Caff.

It took twenty minutes to drag him along Casey Street, into The Caff and to Joe's old room, and he was almost too big for the bed. I took his jacket off before laying him down, its massive bulk covering the chair that sat next to Joe's bed. The jacket spilled over and hung to the floor, a mass of black leather and straps, buckles, weapon holsters, all of which were now empty.

I ran to the bathroom, hoping that the water would still be running, and it was. A few minutes later I got back to the bedroom with a pile of rags from downstairs and a bowl of water. We had no bandages.

As I helped him off with his shirt, and started cleaning up the multitude of wounds, I asked him the first of many questions.

"So, mister, are you going to tell me what happened to get you in such a state?"

He was breathing heavily, but still conscious. I fed him some water and helped him sit up against the back of the bed. I noticed that as well as the wounds, his upper body was covered almost entirely in scars. They were long ones that looked like knife wounds, rows of aligned curves that could have been claw marks, bullet scars, burns, and some that I couldn't have placed. Most looked old, but some were barely healed. Where his skin wasn't covered in scars it was a mosaic of tattoos. His entire body apart from his head had been turned into some bizarre tapestry of images, all of them depicting strange glyphs and symbols of which I had no knowledge. Although this was unusual, and I had never seen anything like it before, it wasn't the most disturbing thing about him. As I cleaned up each cut or hole and moved on to another one, I could see them healing. I mean actually see the blood drying and the skin knitting itself back together. One of the cuts on his chest, that I had cleaned first, was now almost completely gone, in just minutes. He was healing at a rate that defied nature.

"I lost a fight."

"I'll say. You are lucky to be alive."

"I've lost before."

Silence.

I finished cleaning up the last of the wounds. A big slash that split his shoulder muscle on his left side clean in two was closing up as I watched. The warm water seemed to aid the speed of healing. I think he could sense my unease, sense my questions waiting.

"You would be safer not knowing," he said, looking me in the eyes. We stood there for a moment, eyes locked. He had that same serious, cold expression that I had seen through the mist those many years ago.

"I'd like to know."

"Why?"

"Because I have wondered about you every day of my life since that day in the trenches, wondered about who you were, and who that terrible creature was that you followed. How those dead men rose that day, and where they all disappeared to."

"You may wish you had never asked. You may not be able to understand…"

"I would take that risk gladly."

"You do not know what you ask."

"I do, mister. I have seen some damn strange things in my life, most of which went unanswered, unexplained, and most of which still plague me in my dreams at night."

I sat down on the side of the bed and looked away, out of the window, the edges of the broken glass jutting out like teeth, just like those razor edges that had lined the split in that man's face in the trenches, that demon thing whose image woke me up most nights. He watched me, the stranger, as I sat there, his expression calculating. I guess he was wondering whether telling me anything was worth his time, not that I would presume to know what this strange man was thinking.

"Mister, I have never met anyone like you," I continued, "and I probably never will again. And since I'm helping you, rather than leaving you to die in the road while other folks around this way would have just robbed you and cut your throat, since I'm doing that for you, maybe you might consider helping me to rid myself of my nightmares."

He nodded.

"I will be gone by the morning," he said, shifting

his weight so that he was leaning on his side. "That is all the time I will need to heal. I do not need to sleep. As you have helped me, I will help you. You have until the dawn. Ask your questions."

What do you ask first when you are faced with a man who might know the answers to all of the questions in your life? Where do you start? Suddenly I realised that I couldn't think of half of what I wanted him to tell me about. So I just started where it seemed simplest.

"Who are you?"

"My name is Andre."

"Andre? That sounds what Russian, Polish?"

"Let's just say I'm Russian, that's close enough. I was only born there. My path changed when I was very young."

"I see, yes, okay, well, what were you doing in the alley, what happened to you for you to get beaten up so badly?"

"My enemy, the one who I hunt, beat me in a fight. I thought that I was prepared and that I had him off his guard, but I was wrong. He had help. I had to flee, and barely escaped with my life. I was foolish to attempt to defeat him alone."

"Who is he? This enemy? The thing with the scar down his face?"

"He is called Nua'lath, and he is an old one, one of the few that remain awake, an ancient evil."

"Awake?"

"Most of his kin are long dead, or in a coma."

"Nua'lath, is he some sort of a demon or devil then?"

"That is the closest that I would describe him to you, yes, but that is not what he is. For your understanding I would say he was a demon."

"The dead men, the ones that rose from the ground, in the trenches that day, how did that happen? Why didn't they just stay dead?"

"Nua'lath raised them, though they did not have to be dead for him to do so. He merely exerted his will upon them, and relieved them of their souls, so that his minions could take the bodies. You are lucky he did not do the same to you."

"Why did it not happen to me?"

"I do not know."

"You don't know why he chose not to?"

"He may not have chosen. There may have been some other reason. Were you there when the men fell?"

"No."

"Then that may be why. You must have arrived just after he absolved them."

"Absolved?"

"Absolved their souls, destroyed them utterly."

"But they move still, they talk."

"They are but a shadow of what they once were, and twisted beyond recognition. Once their souls have been absolved they become minions to his will, and his evil permeates through them."

"Would you like a drink? I think I need one."

"Yes."

As he had promised, when I awoke the next morning, after hours of questions, and many answers, he was gone. I had slept after we talked, without waking once, on a spare mattress that I found. For the first time since those days in France, I had a night of sleep without interruption.

All that was left behind to prove to me that he had been here were bloody rags, all heaped in a pile on the chair, and strewn across the floor, and one other thing. One more item he had left behind, something that I don't know if he intended to leave. Or if he did, then his reason for doing so was beyond me.

It was a knife, and it had a wicked-looking blade, and a bone handle. The curve of the blade was unmistakable, the small, curved serrations unique, and it was still as sharp today as it had been all those years ago.

It was the knife that I gutted Eddie with when I was eight years old, and all that was missing was the leather holder.

How had Andre come upon this knife? I have no idea, and you know the irony of it was that after an evening full of questions and answers, he managed to leave me with something burning in the back of my mind. Had he been in The Warehouse that night? Had he seen what I had done? Had he recognised me after all this time? Or had some bizarre twist of fate had that knife fall out of his pocket to be left to me once more?

It didn't matter.

It was mine again, and I sat there on that blood-soaked bed for what seemed an age looking at the thing. It brought back all my memories from that difficult time in my life, the Holcrofts, the other families I had lived with, right back to my aunt.

In a room in the middle of a place that I hated to call the closest thing to home, on a street that had a history as long and dark as the alleyways that ran through it, I sat and cried for the second time in my life. The first time had been for Marie, whom I had lost, and now I cried for everyone else.

But after a few moments, the tears were no longer born of pain and regret, they were tears of hopeful joy, born from the new knowledge I had gained speaking to the stranger.

You see, I hadn't just found out who he was that last night on Casey Street, not in the least. The questions had gone on for hours after I brought him back that drink, and another a little later on, a double of whiskey that I found in the back of Joe's office, with a pour of water from the tap.

He had coughed as he threw the whole drink back, and then I began to ask the real questions, the ones that would give me answers I really craved, the ones that could change my life.

The stranger, Andre, had sat there on that bed, his wounds gradually vanishing before my eyes to become yet more scars on his already ruined skin, and as the night slowly passed, he listened patiently to everything that I cared to pour out at him, and he answered everything I asked him as best he could.

Every question.

He answered them all.

"There are other places aren't there? Places other than this world?"

"Yes, there are many."

"Is that where you followed Nua'lath, to another place?"

"Yes, I followed him to another world. I have followed him to many places."

"How do you go to those places? How could I go to those places?"

"You are a mortal, my friend. You could not open the way to other places without help. I am not one of your kind."

"You're not human?"

"I was human once, but not now."

"I don't understand."

"I said that you probably wouldn't. Let us just say that I was once like you, a mortal human, but I have changed. That is all I am willing to answer about this."

"Understood."

"My wife. She disappeared, just like that, years ago, right in front of my eyes. How could such a thing come to be?"

"Did she step through something visible? Was there a change in the air around her?"

"No, nothing, she just vanished."

"Then I would say that she did not travel to another place. I would guess that someone had a hand in her disappearance. Without more detail, I cannot help. But if you wish to find her, I would first try to discover who would want to teleport her away from you."

"Teleport?"

"It is a means of travelling from one place to another, instantly."

"But, I don't know anyone who would want to do that."

"Then you may have to accept that you might never discover this."

"This creature, Nua'lath. Could he have had something to do with it?"

"Very doubtful. Nua'lath would have very little interest in removing one individual. His activities are on a much grander scale."

"How so?"

"You cannot conquer and destroy worlds with just one minion."

"He has conquered worlds?"

"Yes."

"What? Entire worlds?"

"He has destroyed more worlds than you could imagine, and stripped them of nearly every form of life."

"And he is here now, in my world?"

"No. He has merely visited this world a number of times to increase the numbers in his army."

"How many people has he taken from here?"

"Millions. The war that you were fighting provided countless new recruits to his army. There have been many times in your people's history that vast numbers have been taken."

"Just how big is his army, Andre?"

"If you were to take every person that has ever lived on your planet and placed them together, you may have something close to the number of his minions."

"And you fight these alone?"

"No, I am not the only one. There are many, but we do not fight as an army. There are not enough of us anymore. Once we were one of the greatest forces in existence. Now, most of my brothers and sisters stand amongst the army of Nua'lath."

"They defected?"

"No, they died, and were reborn as more of his abominations."

"Why, Andre? Why do you still fight him, when it seems to me that you stand little chance against so many?"

"If I do not, then he will one day find a way to awaken his kin. When that happens, nothing will stand against him."

You know I don't remember at what point it was that I lost that knife. I generally have the most vivid of memories, but that is one thing I can't place.

# 9

It would seem that I am to go home. I no longer have to sit in this hospital. Part of me is happy with that, but part of me is strangely sad.

You know, there is a nurse on the ward who reminds me so much of Marie. She doesn't look like her, but she has the same bright eyes and the same smile. Most mornings she is there, making her rounds. She visits all of the patients to see how they are doing. She came to visit me this morning, but she was with one of the doctors. I should have been listening to the doctor as he told me that they were going to release me, let me go home, as I had requested. I nodded a few times, but really I was only paying attention to the nurse. I was going home, which was really where I wanted to see out my last days, not rotting here in this hospital bed, but I would miss seeing that nurse every morning. You know what I think she really reminds me of? I think it is of a painting that I saw of Marie, many years later.

In 1934 I sold the shop and the yard at the back for what could be considered a small fortune. I was a very wealthy man.

People I knew asked me why I suddenly sold the business and the building and moved clear out of

London, to the north, to Northamptonshire to be precise. Well I saw something in a newspaper that steered my life in a completely different direction.

I was sitting in the office just at the back of the shop, reading a newspaper, when I turned the page, and there, looking back at me, was a young woman's face. She looked a little different, maybe just a couple of years older than when I had last seen her, but there was no mistaking those long dark locks and the curve of her chin, and those deep, penetrating eyes.

It was a picture of Marie.

Marie, who had been lost to me for more than a decade, was staring back at me from the frame of a black and white painting. How she got to be in a painting that was up for auction in one of the most prestigious art galleries in London was something that took me quite a time to track down, but I did eventually.

I started with the auction house, bidding on the painting. I couldn't let just anyone have the picture, the one with Marie's face on it, the one that was simply called *My Marie*.

It had to belong to me, as she had belonged to me, but I also had to find out who had painted it, who had thought, had the gall to think, that she could be theirs. It had been over ten years since I had last seen that face on the banks of the canal in Edinburgh, and I knew that much could have happened to her during that time, someone would know the answers, and this was my first clue, somewhere to start, the first real link that I had ever had to tracing her.

The trace led me to the town of Temperance once more. Of all the places in the world, it took me back to that tiny village where I had been born, to the home of an artist, a man by the name of Laurence Miles.

I had to be careful. I couldn't just walk up to his door and ask him where in the hell he had met my wife, and how he'd come to paint her. More than anything in the world I wanted her back with me, but after more than ten years of her missing from my life, I wanted more than that, I needed more than that, needed to know the why, and the how.

That day on the bank of the canal, she just vanished, and almost right before my eyes. There had to be an explanation, and by whatever means, I was going to find it.

Tracking Mr Miles down was easy. I moved into a hotel in the middle of town and just started visiting the local places. Bookshops, galleries, the library, even the heritage centre, which was a tall thin building with arch windows and a door that was much too big for it. I asked people, and folks started telling me with no little amount of pride, about the town's sole famous person, that wonderful artist who lives out along the vale lane. He had moved into the town ten years before, with his beautiful wife.

His beautiful wife?

She couldn't possibly be, couldn't have married again. Who the damn did he think he was calling her his? I didn't show my anger in front of the town folks though, I kept it bottled up inside until I could take my car a long way out of the town and into some woods. That Holcroft shotgun tore apart about fifteen trees, and a deer that was unfortunate enough to cross my path. I had to get it out of me like that, because otherwise I would have walked right up to his front door and blown his brains out all over his drive. Some people might say that is just what I should have done.

So I waited, and I stayed in that hotel. I waited until I knew enough about Laurence damn Miles that I could approach him.

I had the time, and I had the money to do it. Money wasn't a problem for me anymore. I had so much of it from the sale of the shop and the business that I could have lived for three times my life without running short.

Temperance had changed since I was born. Of course, I'd never seen it back then. But I remember my aunt telling me how small the place was, and that she had been glad to get out of it. There had been fewer than two hundred people living there when I was born, or so she said, but now, the fields had been built on. Overspill, they called it. Men returning from the wars, from many different countries, folks moving out of London and heading north, away from smog and the slums. According to a man I met in the heritage centre the town had grown to nearly twenty thousand people since the end of the war, and all because the mayor had said that land was to be cheap.

I went for a walk the day before I knocked on Laurence Miles's front door, along the lane that led up to his house.

Vale Lane, it was called. It was a long lane that led down to a lake, mostly surrounded by farming fields, apart from the circular path that went all around the water. Along there was a boathouse and half a dozen houses.

The same man had told me where the artist lived, up the lane he said, round the lake and you'll see it, perched up on the hill away from the rest of the homes up there. It was up near the forest that spread out towards Wellingborough, the next nearest town, though that was a good three miles away.

So I went on a walk round that lake, passing only one person, an elderly gentleman with his walking boots on and his walking stick banging the ground in front of him as he trudged his way round the lake in the opposite direction.

I asked him if he knew where Laurence Miles lived, and he did, pointed right up the lane not twenty yards from where we were standing, and then abruptly said "Good day to you sir". He looked troubled, lost in his own thoughts.

I guess most folks usually are.

Just up the path, about a quarter of a mile, was the edge of the tree line, the one that marked the boundary of the cottage's land, though I was to discover the next day that 'cottage' was not exactly the word you should use for such a place.

Temperance Vale Cottage had been the first building in the area, and dated to way back in Victorian times. I'm not sure how old it was exactly, but it was old all right, and the building was quite impressive. The man in the heritage centre told me all about how it had been built by the first true Temperance family, the Stensons.

They were rich landowners who had inherited the whole of the valley, all the way to Wellingborough, but they lived in Scotland. Sometime during the Victorian era, they sold up all their land and moved down south, to the Nene Valley. And that was when the original house had been built. He showed me some pictures, sketches they were, of the original house, a vast mansion built mainly of massive, grey granite blocks, with iron-stone eaves and columns. Three floors of monstrosity, and the biggest observatory I had ever seen on a domestic building.

They were star watchers, the Stensons, and Richard Stenson was somewhat of an astrologer as well.

Well, when they built the house, they did just what the mayor had done a century later, and sold off a whole chunk of land over near the flatland that rose from the valley, and this was what became the town of Temperance. Folks moved from miles around to buy their cheap land and start their farming, industries and shops, and Temperance was born, named after the wife of Richard Stenson, Temperance Stenson. There was a photograph of her in a gold-trimmed frame, up on the wall in the heritage centre. To me, she looked like a fine woman, if not a little stern.

As I stood there on the edge of the water, looking up at the cottage, I realised that something was amiss. It wasn't the same place that I had seen in the sketches at the heritage centre, and I wasn't in the same place either. From what I could make out, and my view from down by the lake was obscured by trees mostly, the original grand building had been further down the hill, by a hundred yards.

It made me wonder if Laurence even knew that the bottom of his garden, where I could vaguely make out flower gardens and an old collapsing and neglected summerhouse, probably hid the original foundations of the first house.

I've met a lot of folks in my life, and it wasn't until I was a lot older, in my seventies a least, that people started taking a little more notice of the remains of the world that their ancestors built. Maybe it was because of the second world war, or even the first, and people had lost so many of their family and loved ones that they wanted to keep hold of something from the past. I noticed that. When I was younger, people were far too busy with their own little piece of the world to take the slightest notice of what had gone before them.

So the next day, I took the other path, the main

road, and walked my way to the Temperance Vale Cottage, the new one, the one that the man who I believed had stolen my wife from me years before lived in. I knocked on the door, waited for a few minutes and knocked again.

No answer.

I knocked once more to be polite before I walked to the side of the house and made my way into the back yard.

The first thing that struck me was the view from the back of the house. Even with the thick line of trees that surrounded the whole property, you could see for miles around. As I stood there, gazing out across the magnificent vista, I wondered if it had been manufactured, picked specially by the first owners, as the spot in the valley that gave you the best view. The lake below sat almost perfectly central, with the town of Temperance rising out of the hill on the opposite side of the valley like some ever-increasing patch of dark, scrawling disease upon a perfect landscape. I wouldn't have ever imagined that the original owners had intended it to be like that, but they were so long dust in their graves that it didn't matter much.

The second thing that came to my attention as I stood there was that I was being watched. Not secretly, there was no one peering out of the window at me from behind a curtain, no eyes squinting to see me from the trees - no, as I turned around and looked back towards the neatly edged patio that covered the ground just outside the back of the house, I realised that I had walked straight past a gentleman sitting quietly on a bench that leaned against the back wall. He was sipping from a tea cup, and reading a book, the title of which I couldn't make out. I had walked right by this man, who was now peering at me with a bemused smile upon his face, right past him and stood in his garden breathing in the view.

"Good morning sir," he said, his voice almost too elegant for a man, and much too genial for someone who had an intruder in their garden. You didn't buy a house like Temperance Vale Cottage expecting to have people just waltzing into your yard because they felt like it. But unless he was very good at hiding his outward temperament, he didn't seem in the slightest bit put out or fazed by my presence.

"Good morning," I replied. I had walked up to the house, clutching my expensive painting, wrapped in brown paper and cloth, prepared to meet Mr Miles, the conversation almost played out already in my mind, but that involved a knock at the door and an answer, and now of course I had to explain my intrusion.

"Are you Laurence Miles, the artist?" I asked.

"Indeed I am, sir."

The book snapped shut and he put down his tea cup and rose from the bench.

"And you might be?"

"I'm sorry, how very rude of me. You must think I am awfully presumptuous walking onto your property like this. I did knock at the door, but there was no answer."

He stood smiling at me. I thought he was so pleased with himself that I wanted to punch him in the face right there. Instead I continued bumbling, hating myself for starting off like this, the one with the excuses to make.

"My name is Reginald, Reginald Weldon. I bought a painting of yours from an auction in London."

His expression changed dramatically, which I was glad of, and as I showed him the painting, I thought that I sensed an air of sadness come over him. It wasn't in his face, just in the way he spoke, the way he stood, body language I think those psychology buffs call it. Personally I don't hold with their study of people's behaviour. I learned just as well how to judge the way a person feels standing the other side of a bar.

We spoke for a while, and he asked me some questions about my interest in the painting, and I lied, told him that I just loved the air of it, and the colour, the depth. I had heard those phrases thrown around at the auction, trite spoken by folks with more money than sense, and far too much time on their hands.

He invited me to join him, so I did. This was after all what I wanted, to get to know him, to find out more than he would really want to tell anybody. I think he put me far too much at ease, because after about half an hour, I asked a question that I should have held back for a while.

"I couldn't help but wonder sir, the title, *My Marie*. Was this someone you knew? I can't help but be intrigued by the lady herself."

"Ah, yes, quite a while ago, years ago I painted the picture, she was someone I met and courted for a while, but things just didn't work out between us. She was a beautiful woman, but somewhat lost, she had too many demons on her mind."

"I see, well sir I do like your work. Maybe you would accept a commission when you are not busy? I have never had a portrait painted, and I think I could certainly afford it, if you were willing," I said.

Lying bastard, there was something in there that he hadn't said, but then did I really expect him to reveal all to a stranger?

He invited me into the house. I'm not sure why. I don't think I ever would have, out there in the middle of the countryside, alone, with a sole visitor who you had never met before. But now I think about it, I wonder if that hadn't been why he asked me to join him in the house. This wasn't a man who needed money, and even an offer of a healthy commission for a painting didn't warrant an invite. I think he must have been lonely.

It wasn't until we walked into the hallway that I realised the magnitude of my discovery. There, all the way up the stairs, laid into  gilded frames, were at least a dozen other pictures of Marie. I stood gazing at his work. Even if I had resentment towards this man for enjoying a time with Marie that by all rights should have been mine, I couldn't help but stand in awe of his skill.

"As you can see, Marie was somewhat of an obsession of mine for the time we spent together."

I could bet on that, I knew exactly how he must have felt about her.

"She made a wonderful subject for my work, and although I mainly specialised in abstract landscapes, for a while I changed my focus to accommodate her. She was a fascinating lady."

"What made you decide that this one should be sold?" I asked.

"It was simply the most recent painting that I did of her before she...went."

"Went?"

"Before she left."

He heated up the kitchen stove as I stood leaning against the doorframe, watching him. As I was watching I noticed that his eyes had taken on a glazed edge and his mind was elsewhere. Where...I wasn't sure, but I could guess it had something to do with his parting from my wife. I had to find out just how that came to be, and where she had gone from there. So I decided that my initial plan, a plan involving making friends with him first, was pointless. Unless I pushed the right button, nudged him where it was necessary, I didn't think I would get much more out of him.

"So she just took off and left you one day?"

"You ask a lot of questions Mr Weldon."

"I'm just fascinated with the painting, and who the lady might be."

"Well, I'm afraid that I would prefer not to talk about Marie any more Mr Weldon, if you don't mind. It's personal."

The kettle had boiled, and was now making a drawn-out whistling noise. Laurence picked up a hand towel, and was about to lift it off the stove when I reached inside my coat to pull out the Berreta.

That gun had travelled with me for a long time now, ever since I received that crack on the back of the head down in Gallowshill. I found it strange for a while, and it made me nervous - the thought of being caught carrying it. But I never was, and I had soon got used to the feel of it, and came to depend on it. It sat neatly underneath my arm, in a small holster that I'd had made specially for the job, a brown suede leather holster, rigid enough to hold the gun, but soft enough that it was comfortable to wear. It was always loaded, but with the current chamber empty.

But I didn't have the chance to draw the gun. Laurence Miles beat me to it. You would have thought that with my years of fighting in the war, and living on Gallowshill, I would have seen it coming. I certainly think I should have, but as I watched him reach towards the kettle I realised that that wasn't what he was reaching for at all.

Leaning against one of the wooden chairs that were tucked neatly underneath each side of the table that dominated the large kitchen was a shotgun. He reached down faster than I could react, picked it up, and pointed it straight at me. My hand, just at that moment creeping into the front of my coat at that moment, slid back out to fall at my side. I knew when I was beaten.

We stood there for a long time, me with my hands at my sides, and him holding the shotgun towards me, just sizing each other up, getting a grasp of the situation, before he finally broke the silence.

"So Mr Weldon, what have you really got to say?"

I opened my mouth, but nothing came out.

"Oh don't look so shocked," he said, that same amused smile on his face that he had when we first met.

"I don't know what you mean," I lied.

"Don't play games, Mr Weldon. I know exactly why you are here, and who you are."

He moved round the edge of the table, backing me up against the wall next to the entrance.

"I don't easily forget a face, and yours I certainly remember, oh yes, I remember you quite clearly, though I am surprised that you finally found me. I guess that selling the painting was a small mistake on my part."

"I've never met you before in my life," I said, trying hard to remember where I might have known him from. I knew he had something to do with my wife, and possibly her disappearance, certainly that he spent a long time with her, but other than that, there was nothing else to remember.

"I see," he said, "well it would seem that I am at an advantage after all. You can take your coat off, and put the holster down on the table, Mr Weldon, and if you have any foolish notions of trying to use the pistol I assure you that you won't be successful."

I did as I was told, hung my coat over the back of one the chairs, and slowly, carefully, unclipped the shoulder holster and placed the gun on the table. He was watching me the whole time, pointing that double-barrelled monstrosity at my face. Even though I had seen death aplenty during the war, I had never forgotten that day when I was eight, and how I had been showered with bits of Mr Holcroft. The devastating power of a shotgun was not a new thing for me. If it had been a pistol, like my own, I would have been tempted to draw against him, I was sure that I could have dodged at least the first shot he would have made, but a shotgun? No, everything this side of the room would have been torn apart.

"Now let us get comfortable out in the yard again, if you would still like that cup of tea?"

Back outside, the tea brewing in a china pot that looked expensive, him sitting back down on his bench and me on the other, the one that was directly opposite him, Laurence Miles gave me exactly the answers I had been looking for, and the reason that I had lost my wife all those years ago. It wasn't how I had intended it. I had planned for him to be squirming as I held him at gunpoint, not the other way around, but he told me all the same.

"I remembered your face immediately, Reginald. I don't forget faces, and yours was one that I remember quite clearly, from that day on the way to Edinburgh. Oh don't look surprised, you wouldn't have known me. I was four seats back and across from you and your lovely companion, all the way from London. I watched you from across the way the whole time, or should I say, I watched Marie."

"That doesn't explain how she vanished right in front of me."

"No, of course not," he said, "That really does require some explaining doesn't it?"

He told me to pour the tea, and I did, just as he instructed, a little milk first, then sugar, then the tea, followed by a little more milk and then more sugar. He insisted that this small ritual was required to get the best flavour, and to ensure that the milk and sugar blended correctly. I thought he was a pompous idiot.

"When you went to relieve yourself on the train to Scotland, Mr. Weldon, I rose from my seat and went to introduce myself to Marie. Oh she was quite friendly, though a little shy. I just couldn't help wanting to speak to her. Did she never mention that someone spoke to her while you were away?"

"No, she didn't say anything."

"Hmm, no I would imagine that she didn't want to upset you by mentioning another gentleman showing her any attention. Of course she wasn't used to the attention of a real gentleman was she? Her being from a poor family and used to scrubbing floors in a hospital, and working in a mill. It's a good job she didn't end up selling her body to the highest bidder. Many others in her situation would have."

At the mere suggestion that my wife might have done such a thing, I felt my cheeks burn with contempt for this man who was taking such pleasure in my discomfort. Had I still been that young man who had headed off on the train with his new wife years ago, I probably would have let my rage get the better of me, and would have died there in that seat. But I was older, and stilled my temper for the right moment - it would come.

"Does this rile you, Reg? Me talking about her in such a way? I know it would me, and it riled me for a long time that I couldn't have her. I had the image of her face burned into my mind, haunting me. The fact that a man like you could have such a beautiful creature as his companion, while I, wealthy and famous for my work, had no one. That riled me. That bothered me a lot."

He glanced away for a second, over towards the garden, nodding for me to look.

"You see that shelter over there, the wooden one, just down the path near those trees? Well, It's called a summerhouse, not that anyone for your upbringing would know. Well, she used to love that summerhouse, and spent hours sitting reading in it. I remember it very well, because I used to sit up here and watch her. I don't think she noticed, or if she did, maybe she didn't mind. You see I lived with her for three years Reginald, she was more mine than she had ever been yours."

"But you took her from me, didn't you?"

"Yes, yes I did."

"How?" I asked, spitting my words. "She vanished right before my eyes, just the day after the train journey. How did you think about her for years and then just have her vanish like that?"

"Oh, I don't think I want to tell you that, now do I?" he said, that amused grin returning. I wanted to rip that grin right off his face and stuff it down his throat.

He started to rise from his seat, and pointed the shotgun towards me a little further.

"Get up."

I did.

"Walk," commanded Laurence. He was nodding towards the summer house.

I rose from my seat and began to walk down the path, realising that if I didn't take the chance and act soon, I wasn't going to get another.

We walked down the path, past rose bushes and fuchsia beds in full bloom. Across the other side of the garden was a small pond with a waterfall, a cherry tree growing up amongst the rocky clefts, surrounded by other, beautiful plants that I didn't know the names of. Even though I could feel the timer ticking away towards my death, I couldn't help but think that Marie would have loved this garden, and I understood why.

"Stop."

Laurence's voice startled me back to the present. I was standing at the steps of the summerhouse, and he was barely ten feet away, still standing on the path. I tried to glance around, tried to see if there was anywhere that I could run to, and just as he raised the shotgun, I saw it. Just a few feet away, behind the summerhouse, was a low wall, barely three feet in height but thick enough to block the blast of a shotgun if I managed to reach it. I didn't have time to let him be smug at me once more.

"Well I think that is enough answers for..."

I didn't let him finish. I imagine that he was expecting me to just stand there in fear while he spouted off some more of his patronising drivel, but I had other ideas.

I ran, stooping low round the back of the summerhouse, and dived towards the wall, desperate to reach it before he pulled the trigger. I think that second of surprise that I had gained was enough, just enough for me to reach the wall. I barely made it behind it, slamming into the damp hard earth just as the roar of the shotgun ripped through the garden. Birds rose in droves from the trees surrounding the cottage, the sound almost as loud as the crack of the gun. The top of the wall just above me exploded into a cloud of dust, stones showered the path and the lawn, and I could hear Laurence cursing as he started to walk round the summerhouse.

That was the first shot, and if I wasn't fast enough the second would take me in the back nonetheless.

With barely half a second to spare I was up on my feet and running, feet pounding the earth across the lawn towards the corner of the wall. Behind me, I heard a footfall on the gravel that lined the bottom of the wall. I dived, up and over the corner, and to this day I'm not sure how I leapt what was easily ten feet, over the corner of the wall.

But I did, and even before I hit the hard stone path that ran behind the summerhouse, I heard the second boom of the shotgun.

I slammed into the path, cracking my right elbow and both of my knees on the stone paving, jarring my back in a way that sent juddering bouts of pain up my neck, across my shoulders and down my arms. The wind was knocked out of me, and for a moment the world blurred, the ground underneath me span. I thought I was going to pass out, and all of that running would have been for nothing.

I heard his footsteps on the path, fast and heavy, not the sound of a seasoned sprinter, but the noise an overweight and unhealthy man makes when trying to run for their life. It only took me a second to understand why he was running. He only had the two shells that had been loaded into the shotgun - now he was out of ammunition and he knew full well that I was going to come after him.

He didn't even get as far as the door, let alone into the house where my loaded Berretta was waiting for him. He did get as far as the steps that led up to the patio though, and I was sure I heard ribs crack as he slammed into the stone paving after I tackled him sideways to the floor. He bellowed like a trapped animal, and tried to struggle. It was one thing when he had been facing me with a loaded shotgun, but when it came to fists and elbows I was way ahead of him. Years of living on the streets and my time in the trenches had given me that edge.

By the time I dragged him into the kitchen, pushed him onto one of the chairs and pointed my Berretta at his face, I had nearly beaten him to death. At first I just laid into him, nearly kicked him around his own garden twice, but I soon caught a hold of my rage when I remembered that there were things I still needed to know. As he sat there in that chair, barely able to move, blood seeping out of everywhere it could get out of, his face puffed up and his eyes nearly closed with the swelling, tears running down his face as he begged me for his life, I almost felt sorry for him. Smug, wife-stealing son-of-the-devil-spawned.

As he begged, I forced it out of him, every answer I needed, and with each confession he made I hated him even more, but as I calmed down, and took a seat opposite him, listening to his admissions, I also began to think that maybe he wasn't much different to me after all - just a man who had done some stupid things in his life, all because he felt he had to.

"How did she just disappear?"

"Please, please don't kill me."

"Answer my questions and I may decide to let you live. Now, how did she just disappear, right next to me, into nothing?"

"You wouldn't believe me if I told you…"

"Try me."

"You will think I'm crazy, or lying."

"Tell me, or I'm going to blow your kneecap off."

"I made a deal with someone. Someone who could move people."

"Move people?"

"Transfer them, from one place to another."

"You mean like those science fiction tales, what's it called?"

"Teleport."

"That's the word. I knew I'd heard it somewhere before. Who was it that did this for you?"

"He is, well, I don't know if you will believe me."

"You want that kneecap to stay on?"

His face had gone red by now, and he was breathing heavily. I was still deciding whether I was going to put a bullet through his brain or not, but at least now he was trying to explain.

"I made a deal with a demon. I didn't realise that that was what he, or it, was at the time, and I didn't believe that it could even do what it promised. But then there she was, standing right next to me."

"This was the day after you saw us on the train?"

"No, no, it was three years later. Don't ask how, I really don't know, I never got the answer to that. He...it...was gone, and Marie was standing before me, and she couldn't remember anything, total amnesia, apart from her name."

"She forgot everything? Her past? Her life? Me?"

"Yes, like I said, complete amnesia. Please, could you point the gun away, just a little?"

I raised the gun back up to his face.

"I'll point the damn gun anywhere I damn well want to, and you will carry on whether I do or don't, and if you keep talking, I might not kill you."

"Yes, yes, it's just...okay."

"So let's get this straight," I said leaning forward, glaring at him. I was trying to be intimidating, but I think the Berretta was doing more than enough of that. "You made a deal with a demon, to steal my wife, and she arrived here, three years after she disappeared, with no memory of me or her life."

"Yes."

"How in the hell did you persuade her to stay?"

"I convinced her that we had been together for

169

years and that she and I were engaged to be married. She didn't believe me at the start, but she didn't want to leave the house, she couldn't even remember what was outside. I think she just grew to accept it. We never did marry though, and we were never close."

I watched him as he continued his story, trying to gauge whether he was lying or not, finally deciding that he had to be telling the truth. He didn't come across as being a very good liar, at least not under this kind of pressure.

"Carry on."

"We lived here, in this house, and over the time we were together she relaxed, became more confident, more comfortable, she accepted what I had told her. She never did regained her memories in those early months."

"And what happened next?"

"Next?"

"How did she disappear?"

"She used to spend a lot of time in the summerhouse, reading, I used to buy her books whenever I went to London. As you know the gardens are quite extensive, and there are many places for someone to walk, to spend time just thinking, reading."

"One day she was just gone. I searched the grounds, looked everywhere, and eventually I found her shoes and the book she had been reading, down in the lower gardens, near the pond and the ruins of the old house. There is an archway down there, it's old, part of the original manor, but older still, and it must have been part of a building that had been there long before Temperance Vale. Even when the old house was destroyed, back in the 1820s, that bit still stood. I could never figure out what was special about it."

"That day there was a faint smell wafting in the air, one that hadn't been there before. It was an odd mixture of honeysuckle and maybe sulphur, and all round the archway there was frost. It was a summer afternoon, but there was frost on the grass and across the stonework, just round the arch. She was gone, and I somehow knew where, to another place somehow. I didn't know that she disappeared from you that day in Edinburgh, and that it had been years. Maybe she had been there before. I always believed that maybe she went back to wherever the demon took her from, but that wasn't the case."

"You found her shoes, and the book?"

"Yes, her shoes were on the grass, just in front of the arch, and there were footprints in the grass, as though she had taken them off and walked across the lawn."

"That was three years ago, and the county-wide search went on for six months before they stopped looking. Of course they didn't need to look, but I couldn't tell them that could I? The footprints stopped dead in that archway."

"She's gone then."

"Yes and no," he said.

"What do you mean?"

He sighed, and I could sense resignation in it.

"I don't exactly know how this came to be, but when the demon sent Marie to me, he must have bound her in some way to this place. I always wondered why she didn't want to leave. Whenever I offered to take her into London, or to Northampton market, she refused, always saying that she couldn't leave this place. I thought she meant she didn't want to, but it wasn't true. It just didn't occur to me that she physically couldn't leave."

"She was forbidden to ever leave this house?"

"This house and the grounds, I'm really not sure how far she was allowed to go, but not very far."

He paused for a moment, his eyes taking on that same glazed look once more. This time he wasn't speaking to me - he was talking to someone somewhere else, someone far from that kitchen.

"A few weeks before she had started to have nightmares, visions of things that were horrific. I don't know where they came from, but she told me of barren landscapes, and creatures that defied any form of nature, terrible things. Then she started visiting the old ruins and the lower garden more often, disappearing for nearly the whole day sometimes. I tried to find her a couple of times, but she wasn't there. The first time I was worried that she had left, but she turned up every time, after a few hours or even as late as the evening. She had been doing it since the dreams had started. The last time, the time that she didn't come back, I just presumed she was doing whatever it was that she did down there. I didn't like to ask, I was just happy that she hadn't left. Maybe I should have asked."

"You said that wasn't it."

"Yes, that wasn't it. After she disappeared completely I didn't hear anything for months, but then one night as I slept I heard her voice in my dream. She was talking to me from wherever it was she had gone to."

"And where is that?"

"I don't know. The conversations were never that clear, dream-like. I never heard her in the day, or even while taking a nap, it was always during deep sleep. She only came to me in my dreams."

"And then what?"

"I started having nightmares. I thought they were just bad dreams, but they weren't. Strange visions of dark landscapes, monstrous creatures, just like she'd had before she went, and then I would hear her voice, far in the distance, calling out to me, but I could never find her, never catch up."

"That's all I can tell you Reginald. I never found her in the dreams, never saw her alive again, and never spoke to her properly since that day."

"You're telling me that if I slept in this house that I might be haunted by my wife?"

"I don't know, it may be that she just haunts me, but maybe."

"How did you come to meet this demon that brought her too you?" I asked him.

"He came looking for me."


Sitting in the kitchen, my gun pointing at him, Laurence Miles was a different man, a troubled one. I don't know if he ever really wanted to harm anyone by his actions, or whether his actions had been just the same as mine - the crazy acts of the desperate. In a way I guess he was just like me. His love for a woman had driven him to the extreme, and I hadn't done much different had I? That didn't change my hate for the man, but when it came down to it, I didn't think I wanted to kill him.

"Are you going to kill me?" he asked.

I sat for a while, watching him, as he watched me, trying to decide what to do next. The man had stolen my wife from me, and lied to her, kept her for himself, and probably never once considered the pain and torment that he had left me with.

"No I'm not going to kill you. But you are going to sell me this house."

"The cottage? But it's been in my family for generations. I don't think I could."

"It's your choice Laurence, but that is the price for your life. I will buy it for a fair price, and you will leave, never to come back here. If you don't, then I guess I'll be buying from the local authority when they claim the un-owned land, unless you have an heir?"

"No, no heir."

"Good, otherwise I would have to kill them too. I don't really want to have to wait while they declare you missing and then dead, and trust me when I say that they won't find you."

Two weeks later I moved into Temperance Vale cottage. Laurence took his money and headed I don't know where, back to London maybe, I didn't care. I was just glad that he went. In the end he seemed relieved to be rid of the house, and even shook my hand before he climbed into the carriage that was sitting outside the front of the house, waiting to take him away. My last words to him were a warning to never return unless he wanted to die.

# 10

It was strange for a while. The house was quiet. I'm not sure what I was expecting when I slept there for the first time. A visit from an apparition of my wife, or strange other-worldly dreams? Maybe, but there was nothing.

The second day I walked down to the old ruins that were nestled half hidden in the trees down the slope towards the lake. I hadn't been round all fourteen acres of the gardens yet, and when I came across the old chapel and the family graveyard in the bottom corner of the gardens, just where another path led off down to the lakeside, I was quite surprised.

I had a walk around the tiny, enclosed burial ground, and inside the building. Most of the graves had hard stone slabs pulled over the top of the earth, decorated, carved with flowers and other symbols, but one amongst them was just a simple headstone and grass. Carved into the stone was just one simple word, no epitaph, no last words, just the name.

Marie.

It must have been strange for him, for Laurence, to go through the pretence of burying her even though he knew that she wasn't dead. I guess he had to go through it. Otherwise folks might have talked.

Apart from just two more momentary incidents, my strange experiences ended there in those gardens back in 1934. The first was ten years later, almost to the day.

They don't always tell you everything in the newspapers. They don't now, and they certainly never did back in 1944, during the Second World War.

The accounts were there of course. It was quite a while before I was back in London and able to find the time to read a newspaper, and when I was, the war had torn the city apart so badly that it was difficult to find a newspaper to read in the first place.

But it was there, glaring at me in black and white, somewhat slimmed down and hidden in a small column, right in the corner of the page, dwarfed by the invasion headlines.

I don't think that I was the only one who saw it that day, but I'm pretty certain I was amongst a very few people. You see, D-Day was one of the most chaotic experiences of my life. I would imagine most people who were there would say the same thing, except their reasons would probably be very different to mine.

I was posted the year before onto HMS *Warspite*. I'd like to say I stood aboard that ship heroic and everything, but as part of the ships fire crew, standing up on the deck looking out across the Channel that day, I must profess it was one of the most terrifying and awe-inspiring moments of my life. When you are

177

carrying a roll of fire blankets and a tool kit, it's very hard not to feel small when faced with a sea full of ships, stretched out across the Channel as far as you can see. I was told afterwards that nearly seven thousand ships took to the sea that day, and I can well believe that. It was an amazing sight.

Early that morning, we started the bombardment of the coast. No, not the famous Omaha Beach that all those films are about, though that wasn't too far along the coast from us. No, we were supporting the invasion of Sword Beach, which was further south, and as the time came for the landing craft to hit the shores, we were busy providing covering bombardment to try and pin down that damn defence line that was the bane of the invasion.

I had been in quite a few engagements aboard the ship during the war, but nothing compared to the bombardment we inflicted upon the coast that day.

Just before they sounded the all quiet, and the guns ceased firing, there was an accident up on the deck with one of the ammunition cases, and a fire broke out as a result of it. We got our alarm and went running across the ship as fast as we could.

It turned out it wasn't an accident at all, but when ammunition for the guns was involved we had to presume the worst. It was nothing to do with ammunition when we arrived there. One of the smaller turrets had overheated and caused a bit of panic.

It was as I backed out of the firing bay that I saw

it. The others in the crew were heading back into the ship as fast as they could go, and I was at the rear, moving slightly slower than the rest.

I was up on that small stretch of deck alone, and I caught a glimpse of the vast panorama that was the invasion fleet, all those hundreds of landing craft heading toward the shore. The air filled with a chilling silence as all the support ships ceased firing, allowing the landing craft the space to approach the beaches in those quiet few minutes, without fear of being hit by their own fleet as well as the enemy. The defence guns were still blazing but we were far enough out that the noise wasn't that noticeable.

The fog and the rain that had been causing such poor visibility during the whole of the morning cleared, and the sun came out. For that brief time it was as though there was no war going on, and that the guns that had fallen into silence would never fire again.

This might sound like a surreal thing to experience, but it wasn't the silencing of the guns, or the clearing of the weather that made my jaw almost hit the ground. It was what I saw in the water.

From my position up on that deck I had a pretty clear view of at least three quarters of the water surrounding the ship. I would say that very few people were looking where I was looking at the precise time something I've never been able to speak of before turned up at the Normandy landing.

I can only guess as to why it was then that it

appeared, swimming underneath the ship. And my guess is the sheer volume of traffic across those waters, and the constant booming of the shore bombardment must have roused it from its sleep, because I sure as hell don't think that anything quite like it would have ever been seen swimming in the waters on a nice summer day down at Brighton Beach.

No, I wouldn't be surprised at all to hear that I was the only living human being ever to set eyes on it. Everybody with any sense was looking east, towards the coast, towards where every personal hell a man could have was coming true for many of those brave souls that would take to the beach during that miserable day.

What was strange about our guest? Well, let me tell you this. I think that if you took every ship on the ocean between England and France that day, and you placed them all together and bunched them up real close, the creature that I saw swimming away into the Atlantic Ocean, as quiet if it was just a six-pound cod, could have risen up and carried them all to America without even blinking an eye, if it even had any eyes.

When I first saw it at first, I thought that it was a shadow of a storm cloud, and one that had appeared right out of nowhere. But I glanced up at the sky, and frowned back down at the water, because like I said, the sky had cleared, and the sun was shining. I think it was only the glare from the sun piercing the sea and shining off that thing's back that showed its presence at all.

It was gone as quickly as it had arrived, speeding off underneath the water, leaving just a little back current and a thin white line of foam as the ocean tried its best to handle something the size of a small island deciding to move faster than a ship.

No one from that day on ever mentioned seeing anything strange, and for fear of being ridiculed I never said a word to anyone, I just ducked through that doorway, back into the ship, and carried on about my duties, barely even thinking about the creature until the war was over and I was back onshore in London.

I was standing in Piccadilly, drinking a hot cup of broth and wondering what the hell I was going to do with myself now that the war was over, other than go home to Temperance Vale. I had found the remains of a half-decent copy of the newspaper from a few days after the landings. it was nearly a year old, and I didn't expect to find anything in there, but damn it if I didn't see a small caption, right in the corner.

Local folks along the southern coast and all the way up to Cornwall reported strange tidal-wave activity that lasted no more than an hour. Only a few small fishing boats were damaged.

I guess my friend took a trip all the way round the south coast and then took a left at Tintagel.

You know, the creature I saw in the water wasn't the only leviathan present that day. You can't but remember that beauty of a ship, *Warspite*. She was one of one of the most magnificent things to see.

Did you know there were seven other *Warspites* before that lady sped across the ocean? I wouldn't be surprised if there were more.

She was a strong one as well, with a heart of fire. I heard a few years later that that old girl refused to crawl into the breaking yard and be torn apart. After all she had been through, they finally decided it was time to retire the old girl, but she wasn't giving up, and certainly wasn't being put down without one last show of strength. She grounded herself a few miles from the yard and forced them to take her apart piece by piece.

# 11

The one remaining moment, and it was just the slightest of moments, didn't happen for another twenty-five years, in 1969.

Almost to the day that Marie had vanished on the banks of the canal, and so many years later, I think I caught a glimpse of another world.

I was nearly seventy years old, and my bones and muscles had started to show the signs of my age. For some reason I had taken to using the summerhouse to spend the day reading in. I would take some tea in a thermos, and some sandwiches, and walk the hundred yards down from the main house, to sit there for most of the day. I don't think I ever did this consciously. Just one day I sat down in there and decided that I liked it. I imagine that this is what had happened to Marie those many years ago. She had found the summerhouse and taken to it.

It was something I did most days when the weather was good. Except this one day it had turned cold while I was down there, I thought a wind had come off the lake and skimmed up through the trees, but when I glanced down towards the lake, the sun was blaring down hot as anything. If you had been down by the lake that day you would be roasting.

Then as I turned back towards to my book,

pulling my gown over my shoulders, I noticed something strange over near the ruins of the old house, something very odd.

All across the grass it was spreading, out from where the trees met the lawn, slowly creeping out like tendrils from the central point, the archway.

It was frost.

I put my books down, picked up my walking stick, and hobbled my way over to the edge of the lawn. Once there, I stood leaning on my stick to save me from falling over onto the grass, where I probably would never have managed to get up.

It was creeping out across the lawn, like a living thing, like an army of pure white ants making their way across some vast terrain. The edges split, and split again, long thin tendrils winding their way through the blades and across the lawn.

My eyes drifted upward towards the source, that old archway that had been there almost for ever, long before the manor house, dating back to god knows when. The stonework was so rough and chiselled it could have been millennia old.

The frost had nearly covered the ivy that grew up over the archway. The leaves were even now curling back in on themselves, strangled by the creeping cold. As I watched, the space between the ancient stonework burst into life, the brightness of the light almost blinding, causing me to look away for a moment before turning my gaze back.

There, between those ancient stones, was a view into another place. As I stood in awe, the landscape inside the archway changed. First it was a blur, a wavering mist, swirling and difficult to focus on, but then the mist settled.

All round the archway it was midsummer, the trees and the foliage were still green, life bursting forth, but between that curved stone barrier was a place of cold winter.

I could see a slope, leading down into a valley, similar to the one that swept away down into the lake, into those blue clear waters, but there in that small doorway was a frozen place, one that had no lake, no hills rising across the valley and into the fields beyond, no town of Temperance. No, in that place there were just endless dry, cold plains. The trees, what few there were, were dead and devoid of foliage. The ground was cracked, and frost coated the land for as far as I could see.

And then it was gone.

In the few moments that I had been given a glimpse of another place, in that short time that the door had been open to me, I had just stood and stared, unable to grasp what was before me, unable to act with what little time I had been offered.

The mists came once more, spewing out like the exhalation of a smoker's breath, and then they were gone. I was left standing on that pathway, watching the frost slowly melt off the ivy, off the grass.

I took a careful step forward, wishing that I had

it still in my bones to rush forward, to run through the door, through to that other place. Would I have been able to survive very long? Would I have just died there in the cold? I probably would have, but for a moment I had been given a glimpse of the place where Marie had gone, and I had failed to follow, failed to act, utterly failed to save her, and failed to at least go there and die the way she might have died. Of course, I didn't believe she had even died. I thought that she had gone to that place to escape. To be finally free of her prison, the prison, whatever its nature, that kept her from leaving the grounds of the house. That prison that kept her memories from her.

Had she found them in there, in that barren wilderness? Had she somehow released herself? Or had she just taken a single step away from this world, only to find that the walls were just as high, just as forbidding, as they were here?

That was the last chance I ever had of finding out, and I didn't take it. I was too slow to realise, and too old and frail to move like I might once have done. If only it had happened when I first bought the house from Laurence.

Too slow and too old.

Every day after that, I sat and watched that archway. Right up until the doctors told me that I was dying, and that soon I would be gone. They said it was hereditary, that my mind would slowly go, and with it the control of my body. I don't know if that was true, but I do know that it wasn't how my mother had died. I barely knew my father, so I couldn't know if it was how he went.

I don't believe it myself, hereditary my ass.

My story ends here.

I can't think of anything else to say, only that I have done things in my life that I'm not proud of, and have missed the chance to do things that I should have.

Sometimes life grabs you by the collar and reels you in, just puts you where you are supposed to be, shows you what you are supposed to do, and other times it just dangles the prize in front of you and laughs as you fail to notice. I failed to notice too many times I guess.

Maybe in death I might be with my Marie once more, maybe I can be with other folks that I remember from my life.

Looky and Winter, those two old soldiers from whom I had learned so much and listened to so little.

Joe Dean, who I wished so hard that I could find again, I'd dearly love to know what happened to him. Now maybe I will.

My mother, that lady who gave me life, the one that folks said was the nicest person they ever met, the one who I still feel I stole the life away from. I wish that had been different.

And of course, my Marie, that kind and gentle creature who had, for such a short time, been the centre of my world.

Maybe now I'll get to see them all again, get to see her again.

I don't know how long it will be, but I will welcome it. There is only so much wishing a man can do before he has wished his whole life away.

Someone once said to me that we leave a little bit of ourselves behind with every step we take in life. We leave footprints, and sometimes those footprints cross, the paths cross, and the people you meet at those moments will change your life for ever. I wonder how many lives I have changed, and I wonder if I had turned a different corner at some time, if there had been some decision I could have made differently, that things would have changed.

I have a lot to be thankful for. I have lived a long life. I have met a lot of folks along the way that I liked, and I can still hear my wife sometimes when I go to sleep, can still hear her perfect voice.

At least there is that, I can still hear her in my dreams.

# ABOUT THE AUTHOR

**GLYNN JAMES**, born in Wellingborough, England in 1972, is an author of dark sci-fi novels. In addition to co-authoring the bestselling ARISEN books he is the author of the bestselling DIARY OF THE DISPLACED series.

More info on his writing and projects can be found at

Website - www.glynnjames.co.uk
Facebook - www.facebook.com/glynnjamesfiction
Goodreads - www.goodreads.com/GlynnJames

Proof

Made in the USA
Charleston, SC
19 July 2014